SAVED
BY HER BEAR

BLACK RIDGE BEARS BOOK 3

FELICITY HEATON

THE BLACK RIDGE BEARS SERIES

Book 1: Stolen by her Bear

Book 2: Rescued by her Bear

Book 3: Saved by her Bear

Book 4: Unleashed by her Bear

Book 5: Awakened by her Bear

The Black Ridge Bears series is part of the Eternal Mates World, which includes the Eternal Mates series, Cougar Creek Mates series, and the London Vampires series.

Discover more available paranormal romance books at:
http://www.felicityheaton.com

Or sign up to my mailing list to receive a FREE vampire romance ebook, learn about new titles, be eligible for special subscriber-only giveaways, and read exclusive content including short stories:
http://ml.felicityheaton.com/mailinglist

CHAPTER 1

Knox moved swiftly through the valley, following the edge of the mountain south, remaining far away enough from Black Ridge and Cougar Creek that he wouldn't draw the people he was hunting there. He wasn't sure whether they had made it to the valley yet, wasn't sure if they were still on their way here, but he was sure of something.

Wherever they were, he was going to intercept them and deal with them.

He sprinted through the dense pines, moving as silently as he could manage, not wanting to make his targets aware of him. Stealth was key until he knew what he was dealing with. Moving quietly wasn't an easy feat for him though. At six-five and a good three hundred pounds of muscle, every damned stride he landed felt as if it was shaking the earth and alerting the occupants of the wintry forest to his presence.

For once, being a bear shifter was a bad thing.

He wasn't fleet-footed like the cougar shifters at the Creek, moved with about as much grace as his animal counterparts, thundering across the uneven snowy terrain.

His senses scoured the route ahead of him, seeking signs of life that weren't animal. If he detected anything, he would slow to a crawl, would slip through the undergrowth with stealth. Right now, he just wanted to get as far from the Ridge and his twin brother as possible, ensuring that the people who were after Cameo, Lowe's female, didn't find her.

Gods, he was going to have to thank Cameo for shooting the human male, stopping him from firing at either Lowe or himself. He knew how much courage it had taken her to do such a thing, had seen how shaken she was by the fact she had killed a man. Lowe would take care of her. He would convince her she had done the right thing and it had been that man or them.

He was also sure Lowe would be able to convince the female not to leave Black Ridge. As little as Knox liked the thought of settling down with one female, he could see his brother was in love with her and needed her by his side.

As his mate.

His thoughts strayed to a pretty bartender and a night two years ago.

Knox growled as his right boot snagged on a root and he stumbled forwards, arms flailing, barely keeping his balance as he fought to find his stride again. He didn't want to settle down. It was the bachelor life for him.

He almost tripped again, huffed and slowed his pace just a notch, because apparently thinking and running was too complicated for him. He jogged past Cougar Creek, checking the occupants with his senses, detecting only shifters and the humans he knew as Ivy and Gabi. No trace of intruders.

Saint, his alpha, would send word to the cougars about their visitors once Lowe returned to the Ridge, warning them to be on their guard.

Knox paused by a tree and pressed his left hand against it, closed his eyes and scented the cold air. It burned his lungs, the chill of it swift to sap the heat from his skin now he had stopped.

He glanced in the direction of the Creek, thinking about the other night when Saint had dragged him to a damned wedding celebration just so he could see the pretty little cougar female, Holly. A female who was now Saint's mate.

His thoughts strayed to what he had said to his alpha.

That he didn't want to be next.

Saint had found his fated female. Lowe had found his.

It wasn't the life for Knox. He liked things simple. No strings attached. No weight around his neck.

Lowe's words echoed in his mind, pointing out that it had been two years since Knox had chased a female.

He shoved his brother out of his head and pushed onwards, stalking through the trees, his mood blackening with each step. So what if he'd had a period of abstinence? It didn't mean anything. Maverick had taken over handling the supply runs into town while Knox had been busy at Black Ridge, helping out with the cabin repairs that needed to be done in the short summer months. A lot of the cabins had needed repairs at the same time, and it had given him no time to get away from the Ridge before winter set in.

He glared at the dusting of snow that covered the ground despite how dense the evergreen canopy was above him. He liked winter about as much as the next bear, should have been asleep right now, curled up under a mound of furs on his bed, not running around in the freezing cold.

An icy breeze swept around him, worsening his mood as it slipped numbing fingers into any gap it could find in his weatherproof black jacket and trousers.

"Damned things are meant to be top of the line," he muttered as he tugged the bottom of his jacket down, trying to stop the wind from getting under it.

Knox focused back on his task as he neared the trailhead, slipped into stealth mode and silently approached the small patch of snow where several vehicles were parked. He didn't recognise a few of them, in particular a small car and a red SUV, both of which had snow covering them. Not recent arrivals then.

He crouched and moved through the trees just above the cars, gaze scanning them, and stopped when he spotted a blue pickup truck that didn't have a flake of snow on it. He eased down the slope, slipping from tree to tree, approaching the vehicle. There were boot prints in the snow around it and the tracks looked fresh, undisturbed by the wind.

He sniffed and growled low when he scented humans. He couldn't tell how many had been in the truck, but it had definitely been more than one.

The only other recent arrival was a black Ford F150.

Maverick's truck.

The tension cranking his muscles tight eased a little at the sight of it and the thought that Maverick and Rune had made it back to Black Ridge. The humans would be no match for the two big bears if they strayed near the Ridge. He breathed a little easier knowing they were on hand should something go down, fear for his brother and Cameo fading, allowing him to focus on his mission.

Knox peered off to his left, back into the trees that covered the rolling terrain of the valley between the trailhead and Cougar Creek. He moved back that way, keeping low, and investigated the treeline. All of the snow was undisturbed. Whoever had come this way hadn't headed towards the Creek.

He spotted Maverick and Rune's trail to his left up the slope and wasn't surprised to see they had chosen the high path. It allowed them to reach Black Ridge without going near the cougars. They must have reached the Ridge before he had left, or somehow he had passed them without noticing. It was possible. As much as he hated to admit it, he had lost himself in thought from time to time during his trek to the trailhead. The two bears could have easily gone unnoticed by him if they had been at a good distance. Their faint scents wouldn't have triggered a sense that he was in danger, pulling him out of his thoughts.

If he had smelled humans though, he would have been laser-focused on his surroundings in a heartbeat.

He swung his gaze back towards the pickup.

Which way had the humans gone?

He focused again, reaching out with his senses and straining to hear something at the same time. All he could feel and hear were animals. The scent of the humans was fresh though, meaning that they had been here recently. Maybe within the last fifteen minutes. Thirty tops.

He broke cover and moved to the truck, placed his bare hand on the hood and glared at it. The engine was still warm.

Knox checked all around the vehicle, trying to figure out how many he was dealing with by investigating the boot prints. The snow was a mess, which made it impossible to tell. He huffed, his breath fogging in the air, and turned in a circle, scanning the snow further afield, trying to spot which way they had gone.

He stilled as he found their trail.

It wasn't heading towards Cougar Creek.

He frowned as he followed it, picking out possibly two or three man-sized footprints and one set that was smaller. A female? He paused at the edge of the clearing and stared into the trees that covered the gradual slope below him, tracking the path they had taken.

Why were they heading for the river?

Knox lifted his head and looked at the other side of the valley, at the white caps of the mountains that towered there, dazzling against the blue sky. The dark pines and spruces that hugged the base of the mountains were heavy with snow too, thanks to the recent storm.

He looked back over his left shoulder to the two old lodgepole pines that marked the start of the trail to Cougar Creek and Black Ridge.

A trail he couldn't see through the fresh snow.

Was that the reason they were heading for the frozen river instead?

Knox pivoted on his heel and stared at the blue truck, part of him wondering whether it belonged to local hunters rather than the people he was looking for. Dangerous people. Members of a drug cartel. It didn't strike him as the sort of vehicle that someone in that profession would own, but then there was a high chance it was a rental like the red SUV and the smaller car he figured belonged to Cameo.

It made sense that they would rent a vehicle more suited to the hostile terrain and climate.

He turned in the direction the people had gone and wound his way down the slope, following their trail. He wasn't going to complain that they had taken a detour and were heading away from Cougar Creek. It gave him time to find them, assess them and come up with a plan before they got that far up the valley.

If they followed the river, it would lead them to the cougar pride. Knox had to intervene before they reached it. He had no love for the cat shifters, but Saint was clearly deeply in love with his new mate and Knox would do whatever was necessary to keep his alpha happy.

It wasn't long before he heard the group. He broke off from their trail, heading to his right, using the shrubs as cover as he approached them. They were moving quickly for humans, covering a lot of ground. He peered into the trees, trying to spot them, and froze when he caught his first glimpse of them.

Knox could tell it was a male even though he wore his hood up. He was tall. Wiry. Carrying a red pack on his back that made him stand out almost as much as his bright blue jacket did. Stealth clearly wasn't a concern for them. Knox hunkered down when another male appeared in his line of sight, heading back towards his companion, and he catalogued everything about him.

He was shorter than the first male, but he was big, his dark grey jacket covering a body that was more fat than muscle, and his face was ruddy, his breaths rapid as he swiped a gloved hand across his rugged brow. He looked like a bouncer. Knox eyed the rifle he had slung over his shoulder. Or perhaps a bodyguard. Knox bet that wasn't the only gun this one was carrying.

He eyed the guy in the blue jacket again and noticed that he had a weapon too, a rifle similar to the one the bodyguard had, only he had stashed his in the side of his pack.

Knox slipped silently through the undergrowth, catching up with them but keeping his distance, seeking the others.

He wanted to growl when he spotted them further ahead of the duo. It wasn't just one male and a female. It was two, both with their hoods up as they escorted the female. She wore a pack on her back and had the hood of her black jacket pulled up too, concealing her face. Unlike the pack the man wore, her dark green one was larger and heavier, had a small pan and a bedroll, together with a water bottle. She had come prepared for the hike.

Four men in total and one woman. Knox didn't like those odds. He liked them even less when the one in the blue camo jacket turned towards the other male and he spotted the assault rifle he gripped.

"I'm freezing my balls off." His accent wasn't local by a long shot. It wasn't even Canadian. Knox pegged him for east coast USA, possibly New York.

The other man, one dressed in a black jacket and black salopettes, looked across at him but Knox didn't catch sight of his face before he was looking ahead of them again.

The leader?

Knox moved further away from them so he could draw level with the two men and the woman without them noticing him. She gripped the straps of her pack and shrugged, shifting the weight of it on her slight shoulders. He dragged his focus away from her and assessed the two males at the back. The tall, wiry one had a blond goatee and was young, no older than thirty. Bodyguard had a good ten to fifteen years on the kid, as well as a good hundred pounds, and was guzzling water like it was going out of fashion.

Knox labelled him as an easy target if he could get him alone.

Hell, they would all be easy targets if he could separate them. Divide and conquer. It was the best plan he could come up with. He would pick them off one by one once night fell. Might even knock them down to a man and the woman and deal with them together.

Shouldn't be too difficult. He would have stealth to his advantage once it was dark and if things didn't go according to plan, he would use his bear form. He was stronger in that form, could easily take them down under the cover of darkness. None of them had night vision goggles.

They reached a steep incline and had to bank right, following an animal trail down to the forest floor a good twenty feet below.

Knox caught sight of the face of the one who sounded like he was from New York and he didn't like the look of him. There was a cold edge to his dark eyes as he stared at the back of the man in front of him, his finger resting close to the trigger of his assault rifle, as if he was waiting for a reason to fire the weapon. A thick layer of black stubble covered the lower half of his face, but didn't quite conceal the deep scar that darted over his left cheek.

Maybe Knox had got it wrong. This was the bodyguard.

His gaze slid to the man in front of him, the only one dressed all in black.

He was good looking, tall, and had his grey eyes locked on the petite female in front of him as he gripped the trees he passed to stop himself from falling down the slope to the ground far below.

"Are you sure you know where you're going?" His accent was Canadian, and there was a sharp bite to it that made Knox feel this man was used to barking orders and having people obey them.

If he had to guess, he would say this one was Karl.

Cameo's ex-boyfriend-turned-drug-lord.

The one who had beaten her kid brother to a bloody pulp and had then come after her, believing she had the three hundred grand her brother had skimmed off the money that had passed through his hands on its way from the streets to his boss.

The female nodded and lifted her head as she turned it to look back over her shoulder at Karl.

Knox froze against a tree, sickness sweeping through him as he stared at her, his whole plan changing in an instant.

Skye.

He bit back the growl that rumbled up his throat and fought the urge to break cover and make a grab for her. He had to dig his emerging claws into the bark of the pine tree to anchor himself in place and stop him from obeying the powerful need to get her away from these men.

He stared at her, heat swift to bloom in his veins, roused not only by his rage and his fear but by the sight of her.

Gods, it had been two years since he had last looked at her beautiful face, but he remembered everything about her—from her stunning rich brown eyes flecked with gold to the silken waves of her chestnut hair, and that little scar that darted across her chin just below her soft lips.

He wasn't sure what she had done to get herself dragged into this mess, but he was damned if he was going to let anything happen to her.

No matter what it took.

He was going to save her.

CHAPTER 2

Skye began to get a bad feeling in her gut as the truck she was in rolled up the snowy forestry track. The mousy-haired man at the wheel glanced at her from time to time, as if he could sense her rising nerves and how close she was to calling this whole thing off.

Behind her, three other men were crammed into the back seats of the blue pickup, none of them speaking. In fact, not one of them had uttered a word in the time she had known them. The only one who had spoken was the man beside her, and what he had said had been enough to not only spark her interest but secure her as a guide.

Something she was beginning to regret agreeing to.

Karl had caught her at a low point. He and his friends had been the first customers she had seen in almost a week thanks to the abysmal weather, and she had been overjoyed to finally have someone to serve, even if it had only been for drinks.

Her bar, The Spirit Moose, was floundering and badly in need of a cash injection after two very short summers in a row and annoyingly long winters. If things didn't improve soon, she would have to admit defeat, and that was something Skye Callaghan just did not do.

When Karl had asked where he could find a guide because he needed to go up a valley to visit his friends, she had told him there wasn't a guide in the area crazy enough to head up the valleys in the dead of winter. With the current weather conditions veering towards another storm and recent snowfall, the valleys would be deadly.

He hadn't seemed bothered by the potential danger though and had asked how well she knew the area. It had been on the tip of her tongue to tell him to find another crazy person.

And then he had slapped a fat wedge of cash down on the bar top, all of them fifty-dollar bills.

She had stared at all that money and had seen the lifeline The Spirit Moose badly needed. It would be enough to keep her afloat at least until summer and would pay off some of her debts. Not only that, but Karl had sweetened the deal by saying that when they returned to town, whether they found their friends or not, there would be another similar amount of money waiting for her.

So she had taken the job.

Skye stared out of the cab of the truck at the valley, at thick white snow that covered the track and made it slow going to crawl along it without plummeting into the trees, and at the mountains that surrounded her.

Now that the haze of seeing all that money was lifting and she had gotten a good look at the four men and had realised where they were heading, she had come to a conclusion.

She should've asked a lot more questions.

That feeling grew as they finally reached the trailhead and pulled up next to another car. It wasn't the only one parked in the clearing either. There were several more trucks and SUVs, and none of them looked as if they had been moved in days, possibly even weeks.

She had heard rumours that there were cabins up this valley and now she had her confirmation. Someone was living up here. Quite a few someones.

"Does one of these belong to your friends?" She eyed the row of vehicles.

"The red SUV." Karl was quick to answer.

Skye wasn't sure whether to be relieved or more worried as she looked at the car in question and found it covered in a layer of snow that had drifted up its side, telling her it had been there during the recent snowstorm but not as long as the others parked further along. They were completely obscured by the snow.

"I said we would come up for the holidays but the storm closed in and we couldn't reach the cabin." Karl offered a smile, one that did nothing to warm his grey eyes. He shrugged. "I'm a city guy. Not used to this method of finding a place. Our friend was supposed to meet us at the start of the track near the highway, but when we reached it, he wasn't there."

Which was plausible.

"The storm blew for a couple of days and dumped a lot of snow. Might be they couldn't get back to their vehicle from the cabin. Do you know which one it is?" She could only think of one cabin up this valley, but there had to be more than that judging by how many cars were parked here.

Karl offered her the piece of paper he had shown her back at the bar. "I only have these to go on. Sorry."

He didn't stop her when she took the piece of paper and studied the coordinates scrawled on it.

"I know the way to a cabin. We can check there first. It's close to these coordinates." She reached into the pocket of her coat and pulled out her GPS unit.

Karl seized her arm. "What's that? Is that a phone?"

She shook her head. "No. It's a GPS. I use it for hiking. I'll put the coordinates in it and we can use it to find our way to them."

He eyed it, a look crossing his face that said he was debating demanding she hand him the device. Part of her was tempted, but she thought about the money. He would probably demand she give him back what he had already paid her too and she could definitely kiss goodbye to the second half of the payment even if he let her keep the first.

"We won't be able to just walk in a straight line to it, of course." She smiled at him, affecting an easy air to cover her nerves and how desperate she was for the money. "The valley has a lot of ravines and areas where we'll have to go around. I know this place well enough to guide you there along the shortest route, no detours or backtracking necessary."

His grip on her eased. "Are there other routes out of this valley?"

She wanted to frown at that question but resisted. "Sure. There's a valley that joins it up towards the glacier. A pass cuts east and you can hike to the next valley along from this one."

He didn't look happy about that as he released her.

Why?

Skye shrugged it off and put the coordinates into the GPS. It revealed a point not too far north from her current position, on the left side of the valley. Strange. She looked in that direction, past the parked cars. She couldn't recall seeing a cabin up that way, but then she had only been to this valley a few times. It was possible someone lived there. The vehicles were proof that people were staying in the valley in the dead of winter, and there were too many for only one cabin—the one she could think of.

That cabin was small. Too small for so many people.

She pocketed her GPS. "It's a way up the valley, but I can get you there. It's probably no more than a day or two's hike. I'd say two given the conditions and how late it is now."

Karl nodded and opened his door, allowing a blast of frigid air into the cab. "Let's go."

The men in the backseat all piled out of the vehicle and moved to the back of the truck. The biggest of the men, a real bruiser who needed to go on a diet, opened the tailgate and bent over to reach into the covered bed.

Skye grabbed her pack from the seat beside her and slipped from the truck, dropping to land on her feet in the snow. She zipped her black jacket up, covering her sweater, and pulled her gloves from the side of her green pack. She left the pack on her seat as she tugged them on and then grabbed it and slipped her arms into the straps.

She glanced at the men as she tightened the straps.

That bad feeling she had grew exponentially worse as Karl spoke in a low voice to the youngest man as he shouldered a red pack that clashed with his dazzling bright blue jacket. What were they talking about?

She eased the door of the truck closed, using it as an excuse to move closer to the men.

"I want everyone on high alert. They might have moved from those coordinates." Karl flicked a look at the other two men.

Skye was starting to wish she had stuck to her guns about bringing her own car and hadn't backed down when Karl had, in turn, insisted that she come with them because they had needed her to guide them back to the track and up it to the trailhead.

She really wished she had when the big man and the one who looked as if he wanted to be in the army, with his blue-and-white camo print jacket, pulled out two high-end black rifles followed by more guns.

They weren't the hunting sort.

She had seen plenty of those in her time and had a lot of experience handling them herself.

No. These were military-grade weapons, the sort wielded by bad people in movies.

Skye had the feeling that Karl and his men weren't here to pay a nice visit to friends after all.

She cursed herself for being so stupid as to think that four men wanting to go up a valley in the dead of winter wasn't suspicious, cursed herself for not asking more questions, and really cursed herself for being seduced by a fat lot of cash.

When Karl glanced her way, she pretended to be busy with her pack straps, kept her eyes off him as she tried to come up with a plan. Running wasn't an option. Her heart thundered at the thought of even attempting it, images of them gunning her down flashing across her mind to have panic prickling her spine.

She was the only one with the GPS coordinates. Karl hadn't taken the piece of paper from her. Maybe she could lead them along a different route. If she headed for the river instead of deeper into the valley, she might be within range of the nearest cell tower. Her phone burned a hole in her pocket and she was tempted to touch it, but knew if she did that Karl would notice. He was watching her closely, as if he was waiting for her to react to the guns the men were now checking over.

Her plan was solid. No sudden moves. No revealing how scared she was. She would make up some bullshit about the easiest way to the place they wanted to reach being via the river and would take them in that direction.

Once there, she would find a way to slip away from them for a moment and would secretly call for help.

She glanced back at the men and smiled at Karl as his cold grey eyes narrowed on her.

Because she had the feeling she was going to need it.

CHAPTER 3

It hadn't taken Knox long to figure out that Skye was in a whole mess of trouble. He stalked her through the woods, sticking to the shadows, keeping his distance so the men she was with didn't spot him. His gaze remained glued to her as she navigated another steep incline, heading for the river.

She knew she was in danger.

That was the reason she was leading the men towards the frozen creek rather than deeper into the valley.

He struggled to tamp down the urge to break cover and go to her, had to fight to deny his bear instincts as he watched her, studying her as closely as Karl was as he walked behind her. When her booted feet slipped and she made a lunge for a sapling to stop herself from falling, Knox took a hard step forwards, his heart shooting into his throat as the need to go to her and help her blasted through him.

When Karl grabbed her wrist and saved her, pulled her up onto her feet and kept his damned hand on her, a different urge surged through him.

Knox growled low, the hunger to rush the man and punch him hard in the face warring with a need to shift and claw him. The sight of the man touching her had both sides of him wild with a need to defend her, to get her away from the bastard who still had his damned hand on her as he spoke to her.

He bared emerging fangs at the male, pictured a thousand ways he would kill him once he had dealt with his lackeys, and he wouldn't be doing it for Lowe or Cameo.

He would be doing it for himself.

For Skye.

He couldn't see her face, but he knew in his gut that she was scared as she gently twisted her wrist, easing free of Karl's grip. She was quick to back off when the male released her, reached for the sapling she had tried to grab and turned away from him.

Knox growled again as he caught sight of her face and saw how pale she was against the hood of her black jacket. It wasn't because she had almost fallen either. Her head turned slightly, gaze sliding towards her shoulder, as if she wanted to look back at the four males who followed her, and then she faced forwards again.

She bravely walked forwards, moving with even more caution now, stepping over roots that snaked across the narrow path that led down into another hollow. Knox lost sight of her as she moved below the level he was on. It was hard to force himself to wait until the last of the men disappeared from view too before he broke cover. He hurried through the trees, heading south from her, to a cliff that overlooked the frozen river. When he reached it, he glanced to his left, spotting Skye and the men a good one hundred feet away through the thick pines. He leaped and dropped to the ground thirty feet below him, landing in a crouch, his ears pricking as he listened to make sure no one had heard him before sprinting through the trees.

Knox stopped when he reached the river, plastered his back against the broad trunk of a lodgepole pine and listened hard. Silence. He reached out with his senses and growled when he placed Skye right at the edge of them. Further away than he had expected.

Still, it made it easier to cross the frozen, snowy surface of the river without rousing suspicion. He eased from behind the tree, his breath misting in the icy air as he studied the river. The snow was deep on it, obscuring the ice, meaning there was no way for him to know how thick it was. The river was deepest in this area, ran swiftly towards the falls just a

16

few hundred feet to his right, closer to the town. Chances were the ice wasn't thick enough to hold his weight, but he had to risk it.

If he got wet, well, he got wet.

He carefully nudged his foot through the snow, clearing it aside so he could see the ice beneath. It was solid at the rocky edge of the river. A good sign?

He glanced to his left, held his damned breath as he spotted Skye on the ice, her head bent as she shuffled forwards. Gods. If she went under... He didn't want to think about it. Banished it from his mind. Skye was clever. Swift. She wouldn't take an unnecessary risk. He knew that in his heart. If the ice looked too thin to bear her weight, she would turn back.

Although.

Knox glared at the four males who waited at the bank, watching her.

Maybe she did take unnecessary risks these days.

What had possessed her to come up into the valley with Karl and his men? She wasn't working with them, that was for sure, and he had the feeling she wasn't happy about the situation she had found herself in— surrounded by heavily armed men.

Had they kidnapped her?

He unleashed a low snarl at that thought. If they had, they would die a more painful death than the one he already had planned for them. He growled again, fur sweeping over his skin beneath his black clothing, the urge to shift strong as he watched Skye. If they hurt her, even laid a damned hand on her again, he was going to get imaginative with their deaths.

Really imaginative.

No one hurt Skye.

His heart whispered that he had.

He sneered and tried to ignore it, but gods, it was true. He wanted to deny it, had spent two years pretending it didn't bother him, but every damned day he had to live with the knowledge that he had hurt her. There was no doubt about it. The way he had left her, it could only have hurt her.

Some part of him had done it to protect her.

The rest had done it because he had been scared.

Now, as he watched her courageously crossing the icy river with four males armed to the teeth following her, he hated himself for being so weak. If he had been strong, had found the balls to face his fears, then maybe Skye wouldn't be in this mess.

He might have been there at the bar to protect her, or she might have been living with him at the Ridge, far away from Karl and the danger they represented. Safe.

Knox cursed and pushed those thoughts away. There was no use wondering what might have been. He had to deal with what was happening now. He would get Skye safely away from Karl and his men, and then he would apologise a thousand times over, until she forgave him for being a monumental dick.

Maybe being her knight in shining armour and saving her would be enough to make her forgive him.

He could only hope.

The last of the men made it across the river and Skye led them into the trees. Knox gingerly stepped out onto the ice and carefully shuffled through the dense layer of snow, sending up a prayer a second to any god who was listening. He had screwed up with Skye, and this might be the second chance with her that he didn't deserve, so he had to make it across the ice in one piece and catch up with her. He had to be there to protect her.

As he should have been.

Knox breathed a sigh of relief as he made it across the river and was quick to pick up the pace. He ran into the forest, reaching out with his senses, trying to pinpoint Skye. The moment he sensed her, that relief grew stronger and his bear side grew calmer, allowing him to focus again. He raced through the trees, closing the distance between them, each step that brought him closer to her easing his tension. When he was within one hundred feet of her, he slowed to match her pace and listened hard. If they talked, he wanted to know what was being said.

The men remained quiet as they walked though. He tracked them for another half a mile, slipping from tree to tree, trying to come up with a plan. He couldn't do anything while it was light, not unless an opportunity that was too good to pass up presented itself. The risk was too great.

He needed to get Skye away from these men as soon as possible though.

Every second she was with them gnawed at him, had him growing increasingly restless with the urge to save her. By the time they began to slow, he was ready to forget the part about holding his nerve and waiting for nightfall and storm in there to grab her.

"We should rest." Skye's sweet voice teased his ears and the tremble of nerves he could hear in it pushed him closer to the edge.

He fought the part of him that needed to rescue her right that moment, told himself that it wouldn't end well for either of them, and eased down behind the trunk of a fallen pine a good eighty feet from her. He peered over the log, his heart beating harder at the sight of her as she bravely turned to face the males and pushed her hood back, revealing a dark green woollen hat and chestnut hair tied in two braids. Those braids grazed her neck and the collar of her black jacket on both sides, and he wanted to groan as he remembered how soft her hair had felt in his fingers when he had sifted them through it.

When he had stood over her and watched her sleeping as he made the hardest decision of his life.

At the time, it hadn't felt difficult. In fact, it had felt easy. It was only afterwards, once he was back at the Ridge, that what he had done had struck him—and it had struck him hard. Gods, he still hated himself for what he had done that night, and what he had done every day that had followed it.

Staying away from her had been hell.

But facing her again had felt as if it would be a hell far worse than the one he suffered daily.

He scrubbed a hand down his face and silently cursed himself. If Lowe knew what he had done, his brother would laugh in his face and then he would sober and say some sage shit like how could he know without trying? His twin would be right too. Knox couldn't know whether Skye would reject him and turn her back on him, not without trying.

Not without taking a risk.

But, gods, it felt as if he would be risking his heart and that heart felt sure she was going to break it.

Damn, maybe he and Lowe weren't so different after all. The only real difference between them was the fact Lowe didn't try to hide his emotions. His brother was braver than he was and had proved that with Cameo. He had risked getting his heart broken and this time Knox knew it had paid off, and it had paid off big time.

Lowe had his fated mate.

Saint had taken a risk and now had his too.

Knox watched Skye as she turned towards the one he suspected was Karl.

"Five minutes." Karl's grey eyes slid from her to the men. "Five minutes and then I want to get moving again."

"Yes, boss," the youngest of the males drawled and shrugged out of his red pack, letting it fall to the ground as he sank against a tree and exhaled hard. He turned to the one with the New York accent. "You need some water?"

Knox scowled at the young male. He sounded mid-west somewhere. Texas maybe? Hell, he could be from Louisiana for all Knox knew. There was a definite twang to his voice though. He had only heard an accent like that in the TV shows and movies that Lowe liked to load his tablet up with whenever he was in town with a good internet connection.

New York shook his head. "Stop fatso from guzzling it all too. We need that water."

The one who looked like a bouncer shot him a glare and took a hard step towards him. "You got a problem with me?"

He sounded Canadian like Karl.

"Yeah, I got a problem with your fat ass. Being squeezed into the back of that truck near you was hell, and you're slowing us down." New York squared up to him and lowered his assault rifle to his side, letting it hang from the strap over his shoulder.

"Patrick. Wade. Shut the fuck up," Karl barked.

Both men locked up tight. Which was which? Knox studied the two men and noticed Skye was too. Was she trying to figure out which name went with which guy too?

"Wade, can you give me a hand with my pack?" She smiled in the direction of the males and Knox wanted to vault over the log and launch at all of the bastards, even when he knew she was only doing it to disarm the males.

The one with the assault rifle and the blue camo jacket huffed and went to her.

Knox grinned.

He always had thought her clever.

She had found out a way to determine which was Wade and which was Patrick without rousing suspicion.

Knox still wanted to growl when the far-too-handsome Wade stopped close to her and she turned her back to him, and the damned human pawed her shoulders as he helped her remove her backpack. He really wanted to growl when the male lingered after taking the pack from her, his dark gaze roaming over the back of her head, heat in it that said he didn't mind her asking him to help her because he wanted to be close to her.

Because he wanted her.

Son of a bitch.

Knox was going to kill him first.

Skye turned and took the pack from him, daring to smile at the male again. She was quick to move away from him though, walked to a spot a few feet away from all of them and set her pack down against a log. She sank onto it and watched the males, her gaze wary. As soon as they were all occupied with discussing something in low voices, she eased to her feet and slipped towards the bushes.

Making a break for it?

Knox moved to intercept her and froze at the same time as she did as Karl spoke.

"Where are you going?"

Skye looked over her shoulder at him. Knox glanced at him too. He had pushed the hood of his black coat back, revealing mousy hair a shade closer to brown than Knox's own blond hair, and his grey eyes were narrowed on her in a look that Knox could only call suspicious.

"Come back. We need to keep moving." Karl held his hand out to her.

Skye looked at it and then lifted her gaze to his face. "I just need to pee. The cold always does this to me."

Karl didn't look as if he believed her, but he nodded and waved her away. She was quick to hurry into the bushes, glancing back over her shoulder from time to time. Knox kept low and moved towards her, coming up with a plan.

It was basic as plans went.

Grab Skye. Run for it.

He eyed her. She hadn't changed a bit in the last two years, was still lean but not skinny, and he bet the thick layers of protective clothing were concealing a body that had been honed by years of hard work and growing up with an adventurous spirit. The toned muscles added to her weight, but not by enough that she wouldn't be as light as a feather in his arms. He could easily run with her tucked against him.

She ducked behind one of the taller pines, using the thick trunk as cover.

Only she didn't relieve herself.

She glanced around the tree at the males and then reached into her pocket, pulling out a phone. He moved closer to her, easing through the bushes until he was only fifty feet from her and could clearly see her face.

She glared at the screen, the hope that had been in her eyes fading. "Shit. No signal."

She glanced around, looking as if she was going to risk trying a different spot, and he inched forwards, a need to go to her surging through him. Now was his chance. He went to stand. Ducked back down again as Wade rounded the tree behind Skye.

The male's dark eyes flashed with something akin to anger as she quickly pocketed her phone, his gaze dropping to her hand as she pulled it out of her jacket.

"What are you up to?" His dark eyebrows knitted hard as he lifted his eyes back to her face.

"Nothing." She flinched at her own lie and the male grabbed her wrist and hauled her to him.

Knox growled as the male manhandled her, as she tried to break free of his grip, shoving at his chest and twisting her wrist. His bear side roared at him to protect her, that this was still the chance he had been waiting for, and that if he didn't do something now, Skye was going to end up hurt. He had to protect her.

She needed him.

He broke cover, keeping low as he closed the distance between him and Wade, and growled as Karl walked into view, heading at speed for Wade and Skye.

"What's going on?" Karl's fingers flexed around the grip of a black handgun.

The sight of the weapon had Knox freezing on the spot and rethinking his plan, because if he launched at the males right now, there was a chance Skye could be shot, and that was a risk he wasn't willing to take. He fought the instincts surging inside him, demanding he obey them, and eased back, keeping a watchful eye on Skye.

"She was up to something out here." Wade yanked her wrist higher, pulling her arm away from her jacket, and reached into her pocket. His eyes darkened further as he pulled out the phone.

He tossed it to Karl.

Karl turned a black look on her. "Who were you calling?"

Skye struck Wade in the chest, finally managing to break free of him, and breathed hard as she rubbed her wrist through her jacket. She turned on Karl, a scowl pinching her features.

"I was calling the bar. I forgot to arrange cover for my hours tonight and someone needs to open it up. It's my business. I can't just let it sit there closed."

Karl stepped up to her as he pocketed her phone. "I need you to focus on the job I'm paying you for right now."

She swallowed and nodded, the fire that had been in her eyes fading swiftly as Karl loomed over her, his grey eyes as dark as thunderclouds. "There's no signal anyway."

Karl looked pleased to hear that as he took hold of her arm and turned with her, tugging her back towards the others. Wade lingered, firmly gripping his assault rifle as his dark eyes scanned the forest. Knox remained still as the male's gaze passed over him, resisting the urge to break cover and launch at him. He couldn't risk it.

He was no good to Skye dead.

Karl grabbed her pack and shoved it at her, and she meekly took it and slipped her arms into the straps.

"We're moving out," Karl snapped at Patrick and the youngest male, and both jolted to their feet, instantly obeying him.

Wade finally pivoted towards Karl and the others and walked back to them.

Knox moved back to a safe distance, his gaze fixed on Skye, silently vowing that when the timing was right, he was going to get her away from these males. He was going to save her. He wouldn't let anything happen to her. His chest constricted as she rubbed at her wrist, her eyes on it, and he could scent her fear.

He kept pace with her, aching with a need to go to her, to take away her fear and her hurt and make everything better. He couldn't. Not yet. She had to endure a little longer. He would get her away from the males. He would.

She sighed and let go of her wrist. She pulled her hood up as she lifted her head and focused on the path ahead of her. His brave Skye. He knew how scared she had to be because he was scared too. He was terrified something would happen to her.

She had a power over him, was the only one in this world who could make him afraid in the way she could. He worried about a thousand things, mostly involving Lowe and his pride, but no one made him feel all-out fear like she did.

He gazed at her from time to time as he moved silently through the trees, his thoughts drifting back to her little bar and the first time he had seen her. He had only stopped for a drink to warm himself up before he headed back to the Ridge from a supply run, but the moment he had walked into The Spirit Moose and set eyes on Skye, he had been done for.

She had bewitched him over a glass of whiskey and he had ended up spending the whole evening propping up her bar, staring at her and talking to her whenever the chance arose.

And he had gone back the next night.

And then a week later.

Every time he had gone to town for supplies, he had ended up at her bar.

And then a few too many whiskeys had led to one of the best nights of his life, and, gods, he still felt like a dick about how he had handled things.

But he had panicked.

He had left in the dead of night without a word.

Scared by what he had discovered and sure he was wrong, sure time apart from her would prove that.

He gazed down the slope at her, catching glimpses of her through the trees that tormented him, were never long enough to satisfy his need to see her beautiful face.

The only thing he had proved was that he was a dick.

Because he felt the same thing now as he had that night when he had held her in his arms after making love with her.

Skye was his fated mate.

CHAPTER 4

Skye tried to breathe evenly as she focused on the path, attempting to shake the adrenaline that had her limbs trembling and heart thundering so hard that it panicked her too. She listened to the men behind her, deeply aware of their guns now and how easily this thing could go south. She was going to wind up dead.

No. She was not going to wind up dead.

It was heartless of her, but whatever had brought these men to her neck of the woods, she was going to help them deal with it and then she was going to get her money and get the hell away from them. It was every woman for herself.

Her plan hit a hiccup as a thousand movies came back to her and in every one of them, the person who had been hired to lead some bad guy somewhere or help them in some way ended up dead, killed in order to tie up all the loose ends.

Christ, she was going to die.

She clenched her fists as she steeled herself and regretted it when her wrist hurt. The bastard Wade had almost broken it when he had been holding her and the look in his dark eyes had said he had liked it. He had liked seeing her in pain.

She risked a glance back at him.

Her gaze snagged on Karl.

He had her phone now.

26

What was she going to do? She couldn't run. The men would shoot her if she did. She also knew she couldn't really let them do whatever they had come here to do. She doubted that this was a visit to friends like Karl had made out. They were after someone.

The adrenaline and fear, and that dash of hopelessness she was finding impossible to deny, combined to make her reckless.

She turned to face Karl and planted her hands to her hips, gunning for confident. "Let's get a few things straight. I'm not buying your line about coming up here to spend the holidays with your buddies. Those coordinates you gave me are in the middle of nowhere. There isn't a cabin near there."

Karl's grey eyes took on a shrewd edge as he narrowed them on her. "And you know where there are cabins up here?"

Bingo. She had known he was lying to her.

"I might." She regretted that too as his features hardened in a scowl and held her hand up, hoping to stop him before he ordered Wade to deal with her. "Listen. I want to know what I'm involved in here. I think I have a right to know."

Karl chuckled. "Do you now?"

She swallowed and held her nerve.

He loosed a long sigh and looked beyond her, into the trees. "I'm looking for someone. The two friends I mentioned saw her come up this way and they messaged me, but before I could come and help them search for her, they went after her. I haven't heard from them since. I'm worried about my friends."

Skye was worried about his *friends* too. "So this is a rescue operation? Why not just call in the appropriate authorities? The search and rescue guys know their stuff. They could have tracked down this woman you're looking for and your friends by now."

"We tried." Karl's sigh was a little too dramatic, giving her the impression he was lying. "They wouldn't fly in this weather. Apparently, there's another storm rolling in."

She wanted to mention that the guys she knew wouldn't have even mentioned searching by air, not for a valley this close to civilisation and with a track that led right into it, and definitely not when the person coming to them for help had a set of coordinates they could use to narrow down the search area.

"Please. We're just worried about our friends. The ones who went after her are from the city." He smiled at her and it reeked of him trying to disarm her or possibly charm her and make her feel nice and safe.

She didn't feel either of those things as she looked at him. He had a predator's smile. It was cold and emotionless.

"You always pack military-grade weapons when you go out looking for your buddies?" She nodded towards Wade. "Personally, I'm having a hard time believing that's for protection from the local wildlife."

"Wade has... peculiar tastes. He often hunts using this gun. It's his favourite. Besides, if a bear came at us, we would need the stopping power." Karl gestured to the two other men. Patrick and the guy with the Texas twang. "Patrick and Cooper here are carrying weapons suited to hunting. Tell me, if a predator was charging you, which would you prefer?"

She wasn't going to answer that question. "Bears are asleep at this time of year. It's the cougars and wolves you should be worried about, and believe me, if you spot a cougar... well... that kitty saw you a good ten minutes before you noticed it."

Karl glanced at the woods again and so did his friends. The sight of all of them on edge was oddly satisfying.

"Cougars get real peckish in winter too. Your friends were probably easy pickings for them." She held back her smile when Cooper's green eyes widened and darted to her.

"That's like a mountain lion, right? They live up here?" He stumbled over those questions, betraying his nerves.

"Yup. Plenty of *mountain lions* up here. Big ones too."

Karl scowled at her and then Cooper. "She's just trying to scare you."

She wasn't. Every year there were reports of some big cougars up in the valleys and some equally as impressive bears and wolves. This whole area was a hotspot for the biggest beasts, ones that put those in the record books to shame. The trouble was, not a single hunter had managed to bag one of the big ones. The only thing they brought back with them from their hunting trips were tales of legendary beasts that had outsmarted them.

Or attacked them.

"If your friends are up here, they're either in real trouble or they've managed to find shelter somewhere." She began to feel a little less scared of the men as they looked around them again. Even Wade looked worried. Cooper looked ready to relieve himself in his pants.

Karl, however, didn't look impressed by her attempt to scare his friends.

His tone was hard and unyielding as he stepped up to her, coming to tower over her, forcing her to tilt her head back to keep her eyes locked on his.

"Enough of your games, Miss Callaghan." Karl sneered at her and unzipped his jacket enough to reveal the gun holstered against his black sweater. "You mentioned cabins. Where are they?"

She swallowed to wet her dry throat. "I mentioned cabin. Singular. I know where one is. It's on the other side of the valley to those coordinates though."

"But you believe our friends might have made it there?"

She nodded because she didn't like her odds of survival if she said she doubted his friends were alive, not if they were from the city and had been caught outside in the most recent storm.

Plus, it dawned on her that knowledge of this cabin was valuable to him and she was the only one who knew where it was. Score a point for her. She had given him a reason to keep her alive and had bought herself time to figure out a plan of escape. The cabin she knew was a long trek from where they were.

"Does anyone live there?" Karl's gaze took on that shrewd edge again as he held hers, his fair eyebrows lowering to narrow his eyes.

Skye tried not to think about the one person who allegedly lived up this valley. She was done thinking about him. She should have gotten over him two years ago. It had been one night—one wild, life-altering night. She huffed at herself for thinking that way and wanted to change it, but it was too late. She had already thought it.

"There's some who live in the valleys, but not normally in winter. If your friends made it to the cabin, they'd be the only ones there." She didn't like how pleased he looked to hear that.

"Lead the way." Karl zipped his jacket up again, a stern note in his voice.

Skye pivoted away from him and started walking, keeping her gaze on her boots as she followed the uneven terrain, picking her way over roots and fallen branches and around the trees. For a heartbeat, she wondered if she could somehow turn the men around and accidentally lead them back towards town.

Wade grunted, "Quit being so fucking jumpy, Cooper."

She glanced back at the men in time to catch the young blond, Cooper, aiming his rifle up the slope.

"I swear I heard something." Cooper swung wild eyes towards Wade. "Think it might be mountain lions?"

She listened hard, straining to hear anything over their incessant talking and the breeze that swept through the trees, numbing her face.

"Don't be so dumb. She was just trying to scare you." Patrick shoved Cooper in the back, making him stagger forwards.

Cooper swung his gun from right to left, sweeping it across her, Karl and Wade.

She ducked on instinct, her heart shooting into her mouth, and then straightened and glared at him. "Calm down!"

"Don't order my men around," Karl barked at her.

Order. Men. It cemented that feeling she had that these people weren't friends at all. Karl was a boss of some kind, and alarm bells rang in her mind as it raced through all the possible ones. Were they in the mafia? Or maybe it was guns? No, she doubted it was guns. They were looking for someone who was on the run from them. Mafia sounded about right. This woman, whoever she was, had done something bad or she had seen something, and now these men wanted to kill her.

She somehow managed to keep calm as that all hit her, followed by a thought about them killing her once they found this woman and had dealt with her. As soon as Skye had outlived her usefulness, she was done for.

So she just had to remain useful for as long as she could, devise a plan and get the hell away from them.

"Your man is the one looking ready to shoot every bird or small animal he hears." Skye scowled at Karl, sticking to her confident act when the sensible side of her was screaming at her to keep her mouth closed.

Cooper proved her point by taking aim at the trees and firing off a round as a stronger gust of wind blew through them.

"Calm the fuck down," Karl snapped at him.

Cooper's green eyes slid to him, his brow furrowing as he kept his gun aimed high. "Something isn't right. Something is out there... stalking us."

Scratch outliving her usefulness being the death of her. This man was going to be it if someone didn't take his gun off him or calm him down.

"Listen, Wade is right. I was just trying to scare you. We don't get many reports of predators up in these valleys." She was lying through her teeth now and she feared Karl would notice it as he looked at her.

Only he didn't look angry with her.

He looked quite the opposite.

She swore she had to be imagining that gratitude in his eyes.

She made a big show of looking around. "See, no predators. Just the wind and a few birds. Maybe a squirrel. Believe me, we're making enough noise that any local predator can hear us a mile off and would have moved on. If it makes you feel better, you can talk all you want. Animals only tend to attack if they're spooked."

Also not true, but Cooper didn't need to know that, not when he was looking relieved at last and had lowered his gun.

Skye turned back around to start walking again and tensed as her gaze caught on something around one hundred feet up the side of the mountain to her right.

Only it wasn't an animal who slipped back into cover behind a large bush.

It was a man.

One she recognised.

Knox.

CHAPTER 5

Knox hadn't meant to be seen by Skye, but now that she had noticed him, he was quick to check where the males were looking. All of them were occupied. Patrick and Wade were working to calm Cooper down, while Karl watched them. None of them were facing the same direction as Skye.

He eased forwards so she could see him again and knew when she had spotted him because she scowled at him, her beautiful face hardening. He pointed north-east with the flat of his hand, gesturing to his right, towards the mountains in the distance on this side of the valley.

A route that would take the males away from Cougar Creek and Black Ridge, into an area of forest that was dense enough to stop the humans from being able to see the cabins.

Karl turned towards her.

She looked away, bent and retied her bootlace, but nodded as she was doing it. Relief was quick to sweep through Knox, soothing him to a degree. He was glad she was onboard with his plan. He watched her as she finished tying her boot, couldn't take his eyes off her or his mind off the powerful need that consumed him. He wanted to tell her somehow that he would get her out of there as soon as he could, but he didn't get the chance.

Karl pushed her onwards, forcing her back onto her feet. "Let's go."

"I have my bearings now." Her tone was light, maybe a little too breezy, but Karl didn't seem to notice. He was too busy looking back at his men again. She started walking, picking her way across the thin layer of snow that covered the ground, heading a few feet up the incline towards him. "I know where I'm going. It's this way."

He was thankful when she stopped heading up the slope and started walking in a straight line, following one of the natural ridges.

Knox scanned the males again, cataloguing everything about them. Wade posed the biggest threat to Skye and to him, but Patrick would be the easier target to take down first. The overweight male was struggling to handle even the slight incline as the animal track Skye was following began to climb higher. Leaving Wade until last was dangerous—the male would form a strong team with Karl—but taking out Cooper second made more sense. The kid was trigger happy, jumpy as hell, and there was a danger he might start firing more than just the one bullet at the trees soon.

The last thing Knox wanted was Skye getting caught in the crossfire when the kid snapped.

Knox's gaze strayed back to her, his bear side growling and growing restless as he kept pace with her, moving with as much stealth as he could muster. It was difficult, but he forced himself to head higher up the side of the mountain, further from her, so Cooper didn't hear him.

He couldn't believe how brave she was as she walked with the men, showing no outward sign of the fear he could scent on her. He smiled slightly. She always had been confident and a little reckless. Those were two of the things that had pulled him towards her, had made him enamoured with her at the start.

The first time he had set eyes on her, she had been handling a fight that had broken out at her bar between two big guys, a petite little firecracker who hadn't held back or hesitated as she had wedged herself between them and separated them.

She had taken a hit from a broken bottle on her chin, but she hadn't missed a step. She hadn't flinched or broken down, hadn't even cried. She had cursed and smacked the bottle out of the hand of the shocked male, had given him hell as she had yelled at him. The other man had been swift to leave while she had been occupied.

Knox had stepped aside for him, had been tempted to collar him so she could unleash hell on him too, but he had been too enthralled by the sight of her bringing a grown man to his knees with threats of telling his parents.

And then she had fisted his shirt and shoved him to the door and out of it.

For a female, Skye had balls.

She had huffed and slammed the door, hadn't seemed to notice the blood that had been tracking down her chin. Rather than wiping it away or finally breaking down, she had pivoted on her heel and begun righting the furniture.

Knox had stepped in to help her, pushing one of the rustic handmade tables back onto its feet and setting the toppled stools around it. One of them hadn't made it and he had turned to mention it to her, the pieces of the stool in his hands. Her large, deep brown eyes had utterly bewitched him as they had sparked with gold fire. They had locked with his for a moment, stealing his voice, and then she had dropped them to the broken pieces of the stool and had muttered dark things as she had taken them from him.

And offered him a drink.

He had been quick to take her up on it, to follow her to the bar and ease onto one of the stools beside it as she had grabbed a towel and dabbed at her chin. When she had slid a double shot of whiskey over to him, he had risked it.

He had offered to take a look at her cut.

And gods, the way she had trusted him still floored him even now. Made him feel like a dick all over again. She had leaned towards him, her black Van Halen T-shirt pressing against the damp bar top, and had let him touch her. He could still remember the soft feel of her skin. It was seared on his mind together with the scent of her blood and everything else about her.

He had been lost in her as he had looked at the wound, inhaling her scent and marvelling at the effect it had on him, how it roused a fierce need to be closer to her. When she had softly asked whether it was bad, he had managed to find his voice and tell her it would be fine, but it was going to scar.

He had dabbed at the cut for her, gently cleaning it, and she had thanked him with a smile as she had taken hold of the towel, her fingers brushing his.

Had rocked his entire world on its axis as she had smiled warmly and told him that 'men dig scars'.

Knox stopped behind a tree as the past rolled up on him and a feeling swept through him, and not for the first time. What he wouldn't give to be able to go back in time and do things right with her. He huffed quietly and focused on Skye, closed his eyes as he pressed his back to the tree.

He had a second chance with her now and he wasn't going to waste it.

His senses locked on to her as she moved below him, passing him, and he wanted to groan and sink into the tree as he smelled her. She still wore the same perfume, one he had never gotten the name of, which was probably a good thing. If he had, he would have bought a dozen bottles and spent the last two years tormenting himself with her scent.

He would have deserved that torture.

Gods, maybe it would have helped him grow some balls and head into town to face her wrath.

He angled his head to his left and stared at her back as she picked her way over the snowy, uneven ground. Wrath he deserved. Wrath he knew was coming to him. He hadn't missed the way she had looked at him. The anger she felt towards him had been right there in her eyes when she had glared at him. She was going to give him hell when they were finally together, and whatever she needed to dish out to him, he would take it, as long as it made her feel better.

But first, he needed to get her out of this mess.

He studied the four males, and then the route ahead of them. There was a gorge caused by run-off from the mountains around seven hundred feet ahead of Skye. It would force her to head towards the river, but at a point where the cabins of Cougar Creek wouldn't be visible. If he could get her to notice him again without being spotted by the males, he could try to direct her to head closer to the mountain instead, where she would be able to cross the stream before it cut into the dirt to form the ravine.

Knox pushed away from the tree and stalked through the forest, keeping behind the males and at a distance from them, ensuring they didn't hear him. The recent snowfall helped in that respect, cushioning his footsteps, but it also meant he was leaving a track behind him. If one of the males cut away from the group, there was a chance they would see his trail of boot prints.

A thought struck Knox.

He grinned.

There was a way to make sure that Skye headed towards the mountain to go around the gorge rather than away from it, towards Cougar Creek.

Knox sprinted through the forest, heading towards the mountain, skirting around Skye and the men so they didn't hear him. When he reached the deep gorge the stream had cut into the forest floor, exposing boulders that easily concealed the dangerous twenty-foot drop to the water below, he stopped and assessed the path that went towards the mountain and then the one between him and Skye.

His blue eyes scanned the ground and he grinned again as he spotted a fallen branch from one of the spruces. He grabbed it and brushed the snow with it, concealing his tracks as he walked towards where he hoped Skye would meet the gorge. He walked from there down towards the creek a little, enough that the humans wouldn't be able to see his boot prints only started at a certain point.

Satisfied they wouldn't be able to see the start of his fake trail, he turned back and walked up the slope, brushing the snow a little so it looked as if it had blown into the tracks over the last few days. He crossed the point where he thought Skye would meet the trail and carried on, following the ravine towards the mountain.

Knox glanced back at his trail, checking it, satisfaction pouring through him. It looked good. Convincing. He continued up to the point where the stream tumbled over rocks on the same level as the forest floor during summer but was covered in a sheet of ice right now. He banked left and stopped near it. Beneath the ice, he could hear water still running, defying the cold weather. There must have been a warm spell before the cougars had woken him and his pride, the temperatures rising high enough that the ice on the mountain had melted to form a torrent beneath the top layer of snow. The speed of the flow was enough to kept the ice from forming thickly over the stream as it entered the shelter of the trees and grew shallower.

It wouldn't take much to break through the brittle ice and get a boot full of water, so he used the rocks to cross to the other side and walked for a few more feet, until he reached a clearing. It felt like a sensible place to stop the trail as he looked around and found several large bushes that he could easily hide in as well as some big boulders dotted among the thinning trees.

Just beyond a bank of those trees, the side of the mountain loomed, golden light warming the snowy slopes and the grey cliffs as the day wore on. It would be dark soon. If he knew Skye, she would pick this spot as a place to rest for the night.

He busied himself with making his tracks disappear into the snow, giving her a reason to convince the males to stop there, and then skulked into the shadows, charting the terrain, picking out spots where he could hide as he ran over possible outcomes. He wanted to take out one of the men tonight. One of them was bound to stray away from the others, even if it was only to relieve themselves. If they were the sort of male who didn't like an audience, then Knox could take them down while they were alone.

Knox rested near a boulder, planting his backside to it, and breathed deep of the cold air, trying to quell the dark needs that were stirring his bear side into a frenzy. The urge to shift was strong, constantly pressing him, but he held it back. His bear side was the more powerful of his two forms and the one he would need to use in order to take down the men without alerting them to the fact there was another male out here in the forest hunting them, but it had its drawbacks too.

When he let the shift come over him, his instincts would grow stronger, his more rational mind suppressed by them to a degree. Meaning, chances were high that he wouldn't be able to resist the urge to attempt to take out all the men in one go in order to rescue his fated female. His instincts as her destined mate were strong enough in his human form, drove him wild with a need to save her, but he was in control, wouldn't let them overwhelm him and make him do something reckless. In this form, he could keep his head on straight and remain rational, thinking things through before acting. He thought he could anyway.

Time was going to tell on that one.

The longer it took him to get Skye away from the males, the harder it was going to be to remain in control. He clenched his fists and focused on his breathing, on resisting the urge to shift and tear through the males in his bear form. He couldn't do that. As much as he hated it, he had to be cautious, careful, and take things slowly. Rescuing Skye was his priority, but he wouldn't risk getting her caught in the crossfire. He couldn't risk her being injured.

If he went thundering into the middle of the men in his bear form, they would start firing at him, and while he could take a bullet or two and survive, Skye couldn't. One stray bullet might end her life.

And gods, he wouldn't be able to live with himself if he lost her because he had given in to his instincts and surrendered control to his bear side.

So as hard as it was for him, as painful as it was, he had to remain in control. He had to. For Skye's sake.

And for his own sake too.

Because he couldn't have that second chance he wanted with her—the future he wanted with her—if he got her killed.

Voices in the distance had his head turning towards the direction they were coming from and his mind clearing as he focused on his surroundings again. Skye. As he had hoped, she had found the trail he had left and had brought the males this way.

Knox ducked down behind the boulder, his vision sharpening to cut through the gloom as darkness fell.

Waiting to strike.

CHAPTER 6

Skye tried not to think about the fact that Knox was out there in the forest, tried not to hope that he was going to save her from this mess, and tried not to worry that he might try to do just that and get himself hurt. He had directed her towards the place she had intended to lead the men, a lone cabin that sat further up the valley, one that, as far as she knew, hadn't been used in a long time.

Were Karl's friends there?

This woman he was hunting?

Her pulse hammered in her throat as she walked. No matter how hard she tried to keep calm, adrenaline and fear had her heart racing and it was beginning to take its toll. She was tired, treading dangerously close to doing something very unlike her.

She wasn't going to cry, dammit. She just wasn't.

Fine, tears might have burned the backs of her eyes and stung her nose when she had seen it really was Knox in the woods with her and not an illusion, and when he had made it clear that he wanted to help her and knew she was in trouble.

But not a single one had fallen.

She wasn't the sort to cry about things, hadn't been for a long time now. She had left that part of her behind, had toughened up in the years she had been alone, making her way solo in this world.

The last time she had cried had been when her brother had died.

Skye grimaced. That wasn't exactly true. She might have cried a little because of Knox. But only a little. Two or three tears tops. She had pulled her shit together and turned those tears into fury fuel, condensing them into a blazing anger that had made her feel a lot better—and a lot worse at the same time.

That rage still burned inside her even now, had roared back to the fore when she had gotten a good look at Knox. Damned stupid, gorgeous Knox. She harnessed it, used it to stoke her courage so she could keep going and as a shield, one that would hopefully make her appear confident and not at all scared of the four armed men behind her. She figured if she could appear as if she was taking this all in her stride, that it could only be a good thing.

Karl didn't strike her as the sort of man who tolerated whimpering, trembling women on the verge of an emotional breakdown. He would probably turn violent with her if the courage she was clinging to failed her and fear got the better of her.

Worse, Wade struck her as the sort of guy who was looking for any excuse to get close to her. She had met plenty of men like him in her time running a bar and could spot the tells. He was itching for a reason to get his hands on her and comforting her would be the perfect excuse.

She carefully scanned the woods, making sure she didn't move her head too much, so she didn't alert Karl or his men to what she was doing. No sign of Knox. Where had he gone? Was he armed?

She still couldn't believe he was up here in the valley in the dead of winter.

Really couldn't believe that he had just happened to run across her, not when they were still miles away from the nearest cabin.

What was he doing up here?

She pondered that as she wove around a tree, frowned at the ground and stepped over the sprawling roots that had broken through the dirt in places and peeked out of the snow. Part of her hadn't believed the rumours that said he lived up in the valley, stories she had heard when he had disappeared on her and had asked around about him. Those stories said he didn't live alone either. A few other men she was familiar with from their visits into town lived up here too.

How much of those rumours were true? Was he alone up in this valley or did others live here too? Did they live together, like some sort of hunter community? When she had asked Knox whether he hunted, he had confessed that he took the odd moose here and there for food, but that trophy hunting wasn't his scene. Maybe not a hunter community then. Plenty of people in these parts came here to live a quiet life away from the fast pace of the cities and towns. Maybe he was one of those people.

Maybe he was in hiding.

She glanced back at Karl, pretending to check whether the men were following her. What if Karl was lying and had mentioned that he was looking for a woman because it would curry favour with Skye and make her more inclined to help them? What if the one he was really looking for was Knox?

Knox had always held his cards close to his chest, had never really revealed anything too personal about himself in the times they had talked at her bar.

Because he had a secret?

Because he was in trouble with the mob or whoever Karl worked for?

Her legs shook at the sudden wave of adrenaline that swept through her and she faced front again, had to clench her hands to stop them from shaking as her mind raced and fear flooded her. If Karl was after him, then she needed to lead him and his men away from Knox rather than towards him.

Unless.

Unless Knox had a plan and meant to take them all down.

Christ, the thought he might intend to kill Karl and the others turned her stomach, but at the same time, a small part of her wanted him to do it. If it meant she survived this, if it meant he survived it, then she would gladly help him take out Karl and his men.

She swallowed hard.

Was she really going to do this?

The sound of running water caught her attention and she quickened her pace, frowning into the distance as she tried to tell where it was coming from.

"Hey!" Karl barked.

She froze and raised her hands, her heart lodging in her throat as fear he would shoot her blasted through her.

Her voice shook as she said, "I can hear water. I wanted to check it out. There's a lot of streams that come down the mountain to make deep cuts in the forest floor. I was worried this might be one of them."

"Fine. Keep moving." Karl pushed her in her back, jerking her forwards.

She resisted the urge to scowl at him and hurried towards the source of the noise. Boulders littered the ground ahead of her and several of the trees started low to the ground from her perspective, which probably meant they were rooted in the side of a ravine.

Skye's step slowed as she approached the gorge, her head canting as her gaze caught on something. She stared at the boot prints that cut across her path, awareness drumming inside her, telling her who had made them.

Knox.

Her gaze tracked them up towards the mountain.

He was probably there somewhere, waiting for her to lure Karl into his trap.

Waiting to kill him.

Was she really going to do this?

She clenched her fists.

She was.

"Over here," she called over her shoulder, pulse ticking faster.

Karl hurried to her and she pointed at the ground. He crouched and inspected the boot prints, and then looked over his shoulder at Wade as the man caught up with them. Wade pushed his hood back, revealing short dark hair, and eased into a squat beside Karl, shifting his assault rifle to his hip. His dark eyebrows knitted hard as he reached out and touched the prints in the snow and then tracked them towards the mountain.

"Might be Jason. They're about the right size." Wade looked back at Karl. "Maybe he was trying to find shelter."

"Or maybe he was tracking someone." Karl pursed his lips as he studied the boot prints, his grey eyes roving over them and then the gorge just beyond them. He looked up at Skye. "Is there a way across this?"

She nodded and pointed in the direction the trail led. "Closer to the mountain the stream will be running over rock and not dirt. It'll be shallow there. We should be able to cross it."

"Might be why he headed that way." Wade looked from the trail to Karl and then back towards the mountain. "It's worth checking out."

Relief beat through her as he said that, had the nerves that had been building inside her, a fear that they were going to see through this ploy, falling away. She schooled her features as Wade looked at her, hiding the disgust that rolled through her as he offered her an easy smile, one that did nothing to hide the banked heat in his brown eyes. There was a darkness in those eyes, a twisted side of him he had revealed when he had held her and had taken obvious pleasure in hurting her.

She looked away from him, lowering her gaze to the trail of boot prints. Knox. God, she hoped he had a good plan, one that wasn't going to get him, and her, killed.

Her nerves began to rise again as Karl pushed to his feet and Wade did the same. Wade stepped to one side and raked his eyes over her. She ignored him and focused on Karl.

Karl swept his fingers through his mousy hair, neatening it as he continued to study the trail, and then sighed and looked across at her. "Is there a chance this trail might lead to the cabin you mentioned?"

She nodded. "It's the route I would have taken. The cabin is quite a way away still, but this guy was heading in the right direction for it."

Karl swept his hand out to his right. "Lead the way then."

She shifted her pack on her shoulders to get it more comfortable and then trudged past him, making sure she trampled on the boot prints a little as she walked. Knox had done a good job of making them look as if they had been there some time, but she didn't need Karl or the others getting a closer look at them and growing suspicious.

Wade stepped closer to her as she neared him, forcing her to brush past him, and she shuddered as they made contact. His hand brushed hers and sickness swept through her as she thought he might grab her, her heart racing as her adrenaline spiked, but his fingers dropped from her. She quickened her pace, trying to put some distance between her and Wade.

She was going to have to be careful around him.

Karl didn't strike her as the sort of man who would stop Wade if he got a little too frisky with her.

Skye focused on Knox and the trail to purge her fear that Wade would try something, slowly relaxed again as she followed the boot prints and thought about the man who had made them. If she saw Knox again, she would find a way to make it clear to him that Wade was the biggest threat to her. She was sure in her heart that he wouldn't let the man hurt her.

Christ, she was sure he wouldn't let any of these men hurt her.

Ridiculous of her considering he had left her in the dead of night and disappeared.

She had no reason to believe he cared about her welfare or that he would protect her and make sure no one hurt her. No reason other than the feeling in her gut—one that screamed at her that Knox would take care of her. He would get her out of this mess.

She huffed at that. She wasn't about to rely on him though. She would keep looking for a way to save herself. The second she saw an opening, she was taking it and getting as far from these men as she could manage.

The trees began to thin around her and she tilted her head back, her gaze tracking up the slope of the mountain that loomed over her. Its white cap was golden against the blue sky.

"It's going to get dark soon." She didn't bother looking back at the men, could hear Karl was close behind her, his boots crunching in the snow as he tailed her. "We should find a place to rest."

"We'll keep going. We need to find whoever left this trail." The way he said that made her feel he wasn't convinced it was Jason who had left the boot prints.

"Your call." She did glance back at him now. "But everyone is looking tired and I don't think it's wise to keep moving in the night. Plenty of wolves in these parts and they like to hunt in the dark."

Not strictly true, but she wanted to slow the men down and she didn't fancy trying to navigate the treacherous terrain that lay ahead of her in the pitch black. She had a flashlight, but the beam wouldn't reach deep enough into the woods to be a comfort to her. The thought of walking in the forest in darkness while there were probably cougars and the odd wolf in the vicinity unsettled her, worsening her nerves.

"I mean, the storm only cleared up a day or two ago and the weather is nice and settled tonight. The wolf packs will probably be out hunting. It's safer to make a fire and remain near it." She looked beyond Karl to the others, and wanted to smile as she spotted how jittery Cooper looked again. "The trail isn't going anywhere. We can pick it up again tomorrow."

"I need to rest. This cold." Cooper huddled down into his bright blue jacket.

"It might be the altitude. Are you from around here?" She smiled at him.

He shook his head. "I'm from Texas. Little place near Stanton."

"I didn't think you were a local with that accent." Her smile widened and his green eyes brightened as he smiled back at her. "You sound like a cowboy. I always loved reading novels about cowboys. Do you know how to ride?"

"Yes, ma'am." He grinned at her now. "I had a horse called—"

Wade stepped between them. "You need to give her your life story?"

Someone was jealous.

Cooper dropped his gaze to his boots and Skye filed away the fact he was clearly lower down the pecking order than Wade in their little group.

"Are the woman and the two friends that came to find her from south of the border too?" She regretted asking that when Karl scowled at her, his grey eyes glacial.

"Keep moving." Karl looked ready to push her again so she started walking, following the trail. "You don't need to know that information."

"I'd like to get an idea of whether or not your friends are capable of surviving up in this valley or whether we're just wasting time." She shot him a black look over her shoulder.

He huffed. "They're capable of surviving up here. The woman in particular."

Skye found that interesting. Was the woman a local? If the woman was real that was. She still wasn't one hundred percent convinced these men weren't here looking for Knox. Why else would he have been out in the woods, miles from the nearest cabin, tracking the men?

She led Karl and his group closer to the mountain and stopped when the trail disappeared.

"What's wrong?" Karl came up beside her and peered at the ground like she was. "Where'd the trail go?"

"I don't know." She looked around, scanning the gloom.

It was hard to make anything out as darkness rapidly approached. She shrugged out of her backpack and opened a side pocket and took out her flashlight, and slipped the pack back on. The beam was bright as she clicked the button, chasing back the shadows, and she swung it to her right and then her left, making a show of trying to find the boot prints when she knew exactly where they would be.

"There." She directed her flashlight beam at the other side of the frozen stream to her left.

She glanced at Karl to make sure he had seen the prints too and then picked her way over the slippery rocks that dotted the ice. When she reached the other side, she waited for the men to join her.

Patrick was last and she tried to help him by shining the light on the stream so he could find his way across. He picked a different route to the one she had taken and bit out a ripe curse as his left boot slipped. His foot broke through the ice and plunged into the water.

"That's cold!" he grumbled as he lifted his foot and made it across the rest of the boulders. He shook his left leg, shedding water onto the snow, and glared at it.

"Did any water get into your boot?" She gave him a concerned look, one that was genuine. With the temperatures so low, having a wet foot for an extended period of time would be dangerous. She had heard tales of people getting frostbite from having wet socks while on a winter hike. Mentioning it seemed like a perfect way of getting Karl to agree to taking a break for the night. "If it's wet, I need to know. You could get frostbite from trekking in these temperatures with a wet sock. Do you want to lose your foot? We can make a fire and get it dried out for you. It's probably best we make sure all our boots are dry and our socks too."

Patrick paled as she said all that and threw a look at Karl. "My sock is wet. My foot feels cold."

Everyone's feet probably felt cold but she kept that to herself.

"We really should take a break, Karl." She stared at him, unwilling to back down this time. "Everyone is cold. Tired. You want to screw up and get yourself killed? Because that's how it happens. You get tired and too cold. Your mind gets sluggish. You make mistakes. One mistake up in these valleys and you're dead. I've seen it happen."

She snapped her mouth shut as hurt rolled through her, tried to steel herself against the memories that rushed into her mind, but knew she had failed when Wade looked as if he wanted to come to her and Karl looked as if he might back down.

Skye turned away from them and kept walking, not caring if they followed her. She needed a moment alone. She sucked down a breath and held it, clenched her fists and tried to purge the pain, tried to shut it down and shut out the memories that tormented her. She hadn't thought about that day in over ten years, and she didn't want to think about it now.

She breathed through the hurt, slowly vanquishing it as she focused on the present, denying the past. She needed to keep her head on straight, couldn't afford to get swept up in her past and the pain that waited there, letting it distract her. She needed to heed her own advice.

One mistake and she would end up dead, not because of the valley, but because of the men. It would only take one error on her part and Karl or one of the others would kill her. Right now, she was valuable and she had to remain that way if she wanted to live.

And God, she wanted to live.

CHAPTER 7

Skye followed the boot prints Knox had left her, shutting out the weak part of her that wanted to feel his arms around her, ached for him to hold her as he had that stormy night in her bar.

She frowned as another beam of light crept up to meet hers, looked across at the man who fell into step beside her, and breathed a little sigh of relief when she saw it was Karl and not Wade.

"We will rest for the night. You're right and the trail isn't going anywhere."

She nodded and returned her gaze to the snow as they entered a clearing, and her eyebrows knitted as she saw he was right.

The trail wasn't going anywhere.

"I think it ends here." She hurried to the final set of clear boot prints, ones that tracked north. "The wind must have blown snow over the rest of the trail."

She looked at Karl. He scowled at the last set of prints, looking far from happy about that, and didn't take his eyes off them as she shone her light around the rest of the clearing.

"The trail is still heading in the direction of the cabin I know." She hoped that would ease his mood, because he looked ready to lash out at someone in a fit of anger, and she didn't want it to be her. "This will be a good spot to rest for the night. Not as sheltered as I would like, but we can build a nice big fire and there's a few logs we could drag around to use as seats."

"What's wrong?" Wade's voice cut through the darkness and she swung to face him as her entire body tensed. He flinched as the beam of her flashlight hit him in the face.

"Sorry," she muttered and lowered it. "Just a little jumpy. Thinking about wolves."

His hard features softened at that and she looked away from him and busied herself with finding some dry wood under the trees that bordered the clearing.

"I'll help." Cooper came over to her and she thanked him with a smile, which set Wade off again.

"I'll help her. You and Patrick clear the snow away so we can make a fire." Wade stormed towards her.

She tensed again as he reached for her, might have flinched a little as he grabbed her backpack rather than touching her as she had expected, because he frowned at her, his dark eyes glittering with irritation. Because she was afraid of him and not the others? They had guns, sure, but none of them were giving her heated looks and none of them were looking for excuses to touch her.

He helped her out of her pack and set it down beside a tree on a clear patch of ground.

"Thanks," she mumbled, not meaning it. "Can you look over there to see if there's any dry wood?"

He looked as if he wanted to say no, but then he walked away from her. She tried to work her way in the opposite direction to him as she gathered branches and twigs, anything she thought might burn, but he foiled her by stopping a good fifteen feet from her and then turning back and following her. By the time she had an armful of wood, he had caught up with her.

"Here, let me take that." He smiled at her as he reached for the wood she had bundled up in her arms and she wanted to tell him no, but he was taking it from her before she could find her voice. His hand brushed her chest as he took the branches, adding them to the pile in his arm, and his gaze leaped to hers and then dropped to her mouth.

"I'll get some more." Skye was quick to pivot on her heel and hurry away from him, her heart thundering and fast breaths fogging the air in front of her face. She slowed as she heard him talk to Karl and realised he wasn't following her.

She glanced back. Cooper had cleared a decent-sized hole in the snow and Patrick had pulled one of the fallen logs out from the trees. The large man was kicking snow away from the area between the log and the fire, clearing down to the dirt, and Cooper moved to help him. Skye took a moment to breathe, steadying her nerves again.

Wade didn't give her a chance.

He dropped off his load and came back to her. "Karl says we need more."

She bet he did. She shrugged and was deeply aware of Wade as he tailed her, sticking painfully close to her heels. For the first time in her life, she bent with her knees, making sure she didn't give him any ideas. She gathered more wood and he took it from her when she stood.

She scowled at him. "This will go a lot quicker if you gather your own."

She motioned towards the trees, trying to shoo him away.

"Karl also said I'm not to let you out of my sight." Wade grinned at her, a salacious one that turned her stomach.

"Then you can gather wood while I help set up the camp. That way Karl will know I'm not going to go running off." She stomped back to the other two men and paused by Cooper before Wade could say anything. "Can you be a darling and help Wade gather firewood?"

He nodded. "Sure thing."

The young man strode towards Wade and she could practically feel Wade glaring at her back, ignored him as she turned to Patrick.

"Here. Let me help." She shuffled with her feet, clearing the snow from around the fire Karl was building. She glanced at his work. A good fire. The man was more capable than she had thought given he was clearly a city guy. She smiled at Patrick. "Let's haul that other log in here too. Then there'll be plenty of space for all of us to sit."

And she would be picking the smaller of the logs, one that was only big enough for two, and she would make damned sure that Wade wasn't the other one sitting on it with her.

She went with Patrick and wrestled with the other log, one that weighed far more than she had anticipated. It took them close to ten minutes to wrangle it into the clearing. She wiped her brow to clear the sweat away as she fought to catch her breath.

Patrick looked as tired as she felt as he sank onto the log.

She checked the fire again. Karl had it going already, the flames catching swiftly despite the slightly damp wood. She turned back to Patrick.

"You should take your boots off and put them near the fire. Your socks too." She stepped over the log and went to her pack, grabbed it and carried it back to him. He bent to untie his boots and she opened her pack, rifled through it and found what she was looking for. A spare pair of socks. She offered them to Patrick. "They'll be too small, but hopefully you can keep most of your feet covered with them, your toes in particular, while your socks dry."

He gave her a grateful smile and took them, tugged them on over his toes and managed to make them reach his heels. She took his boots and placed them by the fire and draped his damp socks over them.

Skye breathed a sigh of relief when she glanced at the smaller log and found Cooper already sitting there, bent over his pack. She hurried over to it and planted her ass beside him, tossed a smile at him as she reached into her backpack and found a protein bar. She opened and nibbled it as she stared at the fire, enjoying the warmth of the flames as they chased the cold from her hands and feet and her face.

"Do you have any more of those?" Cooper nodded towards the bar in her hand.

She glanced at his pack. "There's no food in there?"

"Your food looks better," he muttered.

She looked at the others and caught them all looking at her hand, even Karl. Her gaze locked with his across the fire and then he looked at the flames. She imagined all of them were hungry by now and decided it wouldn't hurt to curry a little favour.

Skye pulled the pan off her pack and set it down on the dirt beside her. She dug through her pack, finding two cans of beans she had been saving for an emergency and emptied them into the pan. Cooper's gaze drilled into her as she kneeled and held the pan over the fire, gently warming the beans. When they were bubbling and hot, she sat back on the log, tipped some of the beans into one of the cans, some into the other, and then grabbed some of the plastic cutlery she always kept in her pack. She placed one spoon in one can and one in the pan.

She offered the can to Cooper. "Share it with Wade."

She stood and rounded the fire, and held the pan out to Karl.

"I'll split it with Patrick." He took it with a nod, genuine warmth in his eyes, and she went back to her seat.

She ate her beans in peace, relishing the satisfied noises Cooper and Patrick, and even Karl made as they ate their share. When she was done, she used snow to clean out the pan and noticed that Karl didn't stop her as she went searching for more clean snow. She scooped some into the pan and hurried back to the fire, and set it over the flames.

By the time it was boiling, the men were done with the beans. She added some coffee grounds to the water, swirled it and then emptied some of it into the only two metal cups she had, reserving enough for everyone.

Skye offered the first cup to Karl and then showed she knew exactly how their little group worked by offering the second one to Wade.

He tried charming her by offering it back to her, but she held her hand out to stop him.

"I'll have some when you're done." She went back to her seat.

It didn't take them long to pass the cups back. She filled them again and gave one to Patrick and one to Cooper. Cooper was quick to drink his and offer his cup back to her with a smile that earned him a black look from Wade.

She poured the rest of the coffee into the mug and set it down beside her to cool while she washed out the pan and placed the empty food cans in a plastic bag and sealed it. Bears weren't awake at this time of year, but it was better not to risk attracting them.

She settled down and sipped her coffee, listening to the murmured conversation and trying to stay awake. As silence slowly fell and the night wore on, she grew increasingly aware that Knox was out there somewhere. Watching her?

Waiting to make a move?

That should have had her on high alert, but fatigue washed over her and her eyelids grew heavy. No matter how hard she fought it, she slowly sank forwards, sleep overcoming her. She would just rest her eyes for a moment.

"Need to drain the snake," Patrick muttered, his voice rousing her.

But only for a heartbeat.

She began to doze off again.

Jerked awake as a harrowing scream echoed around the forest.

CHAPTER 8

Knox was going to take immense pleasure from killing Wade. He barely bit back the growl that rolled up his throat as he crouched in the shadows across the clearing from the group, watching the damned bastard tailing Skye wherever she went. When the male used the excuse of lightening her load to practically fondle her, it took all of his will to stop himself from bursting from the bushes and savaging him.

She managed to escape the male after offloading her bundle of branches and twigs onto him and Knox's breath hitched in his throat as she ambled towards him, picking up more firewood. His heart thundered as he eased through the shadows, moving towards her, a need to let her know that he was there pounding inside him. She didn't look at him though and the chance slipped through his fingers as Wade caught up with her.

"Karl says we need more," he rumbled, almost a purr.

She shrugged but it was stiff, betraying the nerves that Knox could feel in her as she found herself alone with Wade. Her gaze kept sliding to her right, towards the male as she walked with him following far too close behind her. When she lowered into a crouch to gather some broken branches, Wade's eyes gained a heated edge that Knox didn't like one bit. The male loomed over her, his dark gaze pinned on her head as he edged towards her.

Son of a bitch.

Every muscle in Knox locked up tight as an urge to launch at the male and take him down blasted through him. He was alone. There was a chance that Knox could kill him before he could get a shot off and before any of the other men could react.

Skye swiftly stood and scowled at Wade as he took the bundle of firewood from her, acting as if he hadn't been fantasising about grabbing her hair and forcing her to do something.

"This will go a lot quicker if you gather your own." She waved a hand towards the trees, right in the direction of Knox, and Knox grinned, silently urging the male to do as she bid and head towards him.

"Karl also said I'm not to let you out of my sight." Wade's grin was far too twisted for Knox's liking and he doubled down on willing the male to come his way.

"Then you can gather wood while I help set up the camp. That way Karl will know I'm not going to go running off." Skye turned on her heel and strode over to the youngest male, Cooper. "Can you be a darling and help Wade gather firewood?"

Knox wanted to growl at him too and at how Skye kept flirting with the male, even when he knew that she was only doing it to keep one of the men sweet and liable to protect her, and to irritate Wade.

He hadn't missed how satisfied she had looked earlier when she had sparked jealousy in Wade. Knox thought it was dangerous of her. The male looked as if he was searching for any excuse to get his hands on her and she was pressing his buttons, firing him up and pushing him dangerously close to acting on his impulses.

Cooper nodded. "Sure thing."

Wade glared at Skye as Cooper approached him, the look in his eyes increasing that feeling Knox had in his gut, one that screamed it was only a matter of time before Wade snapped and stopped playing nice with Skye.

She went to Patrick and spoke to him, her air calm and unaffected, but Knox could scent the fear on her. The urge to go to her grew stronger when she wrestled with a large log that looked as if it had been left by the last logging company that had come up this way, or maybe it was one the cougars had discarded when gathering wood to build their cabins. It had been stripped of branches and had seen better days, the underside of it rotten as Skye rolled it. She pulled a face at it and rolled it over again with the help of Patrick, and together they manoeuvred it into position near the fire Karl was stoking.

The light of it was bright in the darkness, stinging Knox's eyes.

Skye helped Patrick with his boots and offered him something for his feet. Another male she was keeping on her side. He wasn't sure Patrick would help her if she found herself in a bind, but Cooper would and Cooper seemed close to the overweight male. Knox supposed it was because of their place in the hierarchy of the group. Patrick and Cooper occupied the same lower rung of the ladder, something which was liable to make them have each other's backs.

She stood and pivoted, relief washing across her firelit features as she spotted that Cooper was already sitting on the smaller of the two logs. Knox loosed a low growl now, keeping it quiet enough that no one would hear him, because he knew why she looked relieved—she had feared she would have to sit near Wade.

She was quick to carry her backpack to the end of the log closest to where Knox hid and sit down on it. Wade cast Cooper a disgruntled look as he was forced to sit with the other men instead of her and for a heartbeat Knox feared he might make the younger male move, pulling rank on him, but then Cooper spoke to Skye.

Knox sank back against the trunk of a pine, settling on his ass, and watched her as she interacted with the males, feeding them and putting smiles on their faces—even Karl's. His clever little fated female. Her years running the bar had helped her learn how to deal with difficult people, how to keep them on her side and make life easier for herself. He only hoped that knowledge would help her in the hours ahead of her too.

He watched the males, keeping a close eye on Wade in particular, as the night wore on and they all went from talkative to quiet, even contemplative. Karl stared at the fire in the same way as Skye did, a distant look on his face as the golden light flickered over it. Knox slid his gaze to Skye and kept it there, studying her profile as she leaned over and propped her head up on her upturned hand.

It wouldn't be long now.

He moved to his feet, remaining in a crouch, waiting.

Wondering.

What would Skye think of him after tonight? She had to know he wasn't going to let these men leave the valley alive. She had to know he meant to kill them.

But she had still led them here.

He tried to ignore the way his stomach squirmed as he thought about what he was going to do. It wasn't because of what he was going to do. Killing these men wasn't going to bother him in the slightest. It was because he feared that Skye would run from him, that she would see him in a different light after tonight and wouldn't be able to handle what he had done to gain her freedom.

Gods, he hoped she didn't.

He stared at her, watching as her eyes slipped shut and then snapped open again and she jerked upright. An ache formed in his chest, born of a need to go to her and hold her, to feel her in his arms again. He wanted to tuck her close to him and drop his head to her dark hair to breathe her in and know it was really her, and that she was real, not a dream or a fantasy. She was real.

Knox battled the urge to cross the short stretch of snow between them and gather her into his arms, shoved his mind back on track, because there would be no holding her close to him if he didn't get her out of this mess.

He wasn't sure she would let him hold her even when he did get her away from these males.

That feeling that he was in for it when they were finally together hadn't gone anywhere. If she didn't leave because he had killed these males, then she would probably leave because he had hurt her in the past.

If he told her that he had spent the last two years torn between seeing her again and keeping his distance, would it help his cause?

Part of him doubted it. She would probably call him on the fact he hadn't had the balls to face her. Gods, she would be right about that. Every time he had come close to finding an excuse to head into town so he could see her again, he had lost his nerve at the last second, and in his heart, he knew it wasn't because she was human and he had felt they couldn't be together because of that fact.

He had been soul-deep afraid that she would lash out at him.

Or worse.

That she would be with another male, would be happy with him and maybe even married.

He dropped his gaze to her hands and cursed her gloves. If she took them off, would he find a gold band on her finger? He idly rubbed his chest through his black jacket, trying to soothe the ache building there. A woman as beautiful as Skye was bound to have had a few suitors over the last two years, might have even settled down as he feared. If she had moved on, he could hardly blame her for it.

Things between them amounted to one wild night.

Followed by him running out on her before dawn.

Hardly a reason for her to wait for him.

He was man enough to admit that what he had done had been wrong and that she had every right to move on with her life and find happiness with someone else. The bear in him roared in agony at the thought she might have though, paced restlessly and battered the cage of his human form, wanting out, needing to lash out at everything that stood between him and his beautiful fated female.

The compulsion to go to her crashed over him again, trying to tear down his strength, attempting to push him into action. Resisting it became close to impossible as she dozed off, slumping forwards, and Wade slid a look at her. She jerked awake when someone spoke.

Patrick stood and Knox's senses sharpened, fatigue pushed to the back of his mind as he tracked the male's movements. He pulled his socks and boots on and headed to Knox's right.

Towards the trees.

Knox eased backwards, deeper into the woods, and stripped his clothes off, leaving them behind a tree a good forty feet from the clearing. He focused and let the change come over him, wanted to growl in pleasure as fur rippled over his skin and he dropped to all fours, his bear side coming to the fore. Five-inch-long claws burst from his heavy paws as his face morphed, his ears rounding and moving upwards as his nose elongated into a snout and his teeth sharpened. His more animal instincts seized control, the urge to go to his mate almost overpowering him as they dampened his ability to think about actions and consequences and about his plan. It was hard to control himself and stop himself from bursting from the trees as he glanced in Skye's direction.

He shook out his fur to get more comfortable and lumbered through the trees in the direction Patrick had taken instead, trying to move with stealth, something which was easier said than done when he was a six-hundred-pound bear. He carefully placed each paw, hoping the snow would cushion his weight enough that any branches hidden beneath it wouldn't snap and alert the males to his presence.

Knox growled low as he caught Patrick's scent and spied him ahead, still walking into the trees. He glanced at the camp, ensuring no one was looking his way. They were talking again, Karl saying something he tuned out as he fixed all of his senses on the overweight male he was stalking.

Patrick stopped, unzipped his pants, and grumbled something about the cold.

The cold was about to be the least of his worries.

Knox's upper lip curled back off his fangs as he eased up behind the male, the hunger to strike him down seething inside him, born of a need to not only protect Skye but to protect his brother and Cameo too. This male was a threat to them all.

A threat to everyone at the Ridge and the Creek.

On a low, moaning growl, Knox closed the distance between him and the male.

The acrid scent of fear swamped the air as Patrick locked up tight and started trembling.

The male's breath stuttered as he slowly turned his head to his right, his brow furrowed and his eyes wide as they edged towards Knox.

He screamed.

Knox rose up onto his back paws, coming to tower at least two feet taller than the male, and roared as he swung with his right front paw. He smashed it into Patrick's head, delivering a crushing blow that cut his scream off and sent him to the ground on a pained grunt. He struck again, savagely clawing at the male's grey jacket, raking deep grooves in the material and his flesh to ensure it looked like the animal attack it was. He needed it to look like a regular bear attack to keep Skye safe.

The male unleashed an agonised yell as he desperately tried to fight Knox off.

Instinct seized control, had him slamming his paw into the male's head again, shattering his skull.

Killing him.

His primal instincts didn't release him as the male went still.

They had him turning towards the camp as the voices grew louder, as he scented Skye's fear. His female feared. His female was in danger. It wreaked havoc on him, had his instincts bellowing at him to save her.

On a vicious roar, Knox turned and charged towards the camp.

He thundered towards her, drawn to her, filled with a need to save her. Wade appeared from the gloom and Knox growled as he ran at him, as the male fumbled with his weapon and tried to raise it. He slammed into the bastard, knocking him back into a tree, relishing his muffled grunt as he hit it and dropped to the ground. The urge to finish him off was strong, but the need to reach Skye was even stronger, had him running harder in her direction, determined to save her.

Karl dodged to his right as Knox closed in on him, swift to place trees between him and Knox.

Ahead of him, the clearing came into view.

He growled as Skye kicked off only to be collared by Cooper, the one male Knox had been sure would be on her side. Cooper pulled her back to him, his green eyes wide, his face ashen as he stared into the woods in Knox's direction and reached for his rifle. She struggled, desperately trying to break free of him, fear written in every line of her beautiful face as she clawed and kicked at Cooper.

Knox roared at the bastard for holding her against her will.

And charged at him.

CHAPTER 9

Sheer terror ripped through Skye as a deep growl echoed through the night followed by an agonised yell. She shot to her feet, suddenly very awake, her heart pounding at a sickening pace in her throat and her legs trembling beneath her as she stared in the direction Patrick had gone.

"What the fuck is that?" Wade whipped towards her, his eyes wide. "A wolf?"

She shook her head and tried to find her voice, but the words wouldn't come as a shiver bolted down her spine and another bellow of pain tore through the forest. Oh God. Her breaths came faster as she dropped and fumbled with her pack, her hands shaking so badly that she struggled to get the top open.

"What is it!?" Wade took a hard step towards her and her head snapped up.

"*Bear.*" That word burst from her lips. "A bear. It's a really fucking angry bear."

Just as those trembling words rushed from her, another vicious growl sliced through the darkness, making the hairs on her nape stand on end and her heart miss a beat.

"Oh God. Oh God. Oh God." Cooper wasn't helping her nerves.

"Shut up!" she snapped at him, fear getting the better of her, and cursed when she fumbled with the canister of bear spray she had found and it tumbled from her grip to roll across the dirt to the snow. "Damn it."

"Wait here. Keep an eye on her. Do not let her leave," Karl barked and Cooper tensed, his entire body locking up tight. Karl looked at Wade. "Grab your gun."

"You kidding me?" Wade bit out. "Patrick is dead. You wanna end up like him too?"

Karl levelled a black look on the man, one that had Wade falling silent and easing back a step as he looked away from his boss. "I said grab your gun."

Skye wanted to tell them not to be so crazy, but she held her tongue, denying the urge to press them to forget about trying to help their friend. If the bear killed them too, she would only have to deal with Cooper, and she was ninety percent certain he would let her go.

Her rough breaths filled the silence as Wade grabbed his assault rifle and followed Karl into the trees. The darkness swallowed them and she listened hard, fearing the bear would sneak up on her and kill her next. Beside her, Cooper was looking twitchy again, his green eyes darting over everything.

"We should move," she whispered, too scared to speak any louder in case the bear heard her. "This fire is dampening our vision. We won't see the bear coming—"

"Karl said to stay here." Cooper's voice gained an uncharacteristically hard edge and she glanced at him. He glared at her. "We're not going anywhere. The fire will deter the bear. You said that."

"No, I didn't! I said that the fire would deter wolves. I really fucking doubt that the angry bear out there in the woods is going to care that there's a fire blazing a few feet from us!" She strained to hear what was happening, the hope that she could convince Cooper to move and possibly mount an escape lessening as the seconds ticked past. Her gaze flicked to the cannister she had dropped, a weapon that would probably work better against the bear than the guns the men were toting, and she took a step towards it.

"Stay there," Cooper growled.

She turned on him. "I want that bear spray. You all have guns. I deserve to be armed too."

It turned out Cooper was more loyal than she had given him credit for, because when the bear roared and she heard a pained grunt coming from the direction Wade and Karl had gone, she tried to make a break for it.

Only Cooper lunged for her and grabbed the back of her jacket, his fingers closing tightly around the collar of it to stop her from swiping the cannister from the ground and escaping. Damn it.

She twisted and wrestled with him, trying to break free as her pulse jacked up, as adrenaline flooded her veins and every instinct she possessed screamed at her to get away from him and run for it.

Cooper refused to release her though, dragged her closer to him as he leaned to his left and grabbed his rifle. Skye stilled as the bushes swayed and rustled, her heart close to stopping as her gaze whipped in that direction and she watched with dread as heavy footfalls reached her ears.

No. She wasn't going to die here. She wasn't.

With renewed vigour, she twisted towards Cooper and kicked at him, battered him with her fists as a desperate need to escape flooded her, because that wasn't Wade and Karl thundering towards them.

That was a bear.

Cooper lifted his rifle.

The bear roared and charged at them as it burst from the bushes.

She grunted as Cooper threw her to the ground at his feet and aimed his rifle, covered her head and curled into a ball as fear got the better of her, locking every muscle in her body and shutting down her mind. Cooper fired several rounds towards the woods and she caught a glimpse of an enormous grizzly coming right at her before it shifted course on an angry groan and ploughed into the scrub, heading to her right.

Skye stared at where it had been, her ears ringing, numbness sweeping through her as she kept replaying the few seconds where the bear had been charging towards her.

She tensed again as something else crashed through the bushes, her gaze zipping there and her breath hitching in her throat. It leaked from her as firelight chased over Wade as he emerged from the forest, his assault rifle gripped tightly in his hands as his gaze swung in all directions.

"It was a bear! A fucking bear!" Cooper's voice shook as the end of the barrel of his rifle dropped, falling to rest on the dirt near Skye's feet.

She was quick to sit up and shake off her fear now that Wade was back and looking as if he wanted to come to her.

"A big bastard too." Wade turned in all directions again and the light from the fire caught on the blood that tracked down the side of his head. "Smashed me into a tree. Came running towards here like it was on a fucking mission."

His gaze slid to her and lingered, the hard edge to his eyes softening.

"You okay?" Wade's brow furrowed and he grimaced, removed his left hand from his rifle and lifted it. He gingerly pressed his fingers to the wound on his forehead. "Shit, that hurts."

"I thought bears slept through winter?" Karl strode towards her, looking like a man on a mission, and she shuffled backwards, fearing he would lash out at her because the bear had frightened him.

She had seen plenty of men act like that in the past. Some men reacted to being scared by something with violence, as if fear was a weakness and they didn't want anyone to think them weak, so they lashed out at everyone who was near them.

Normally picked on the weakest person in the area to make themselves look strong.

Skye swallowed her fear and gripped the log as her back hit it. She pulled herself up onto it and refused to let him intimidate her, stared him down as she pulled her shit together.

"It must have been disturbed. Bears sleep through winter, but we're not exactly being subtle." She dusted her black jacket off and glared up at the blond man next to her. "Cooper shot up that tree pretty good a few hours ago. It might have been enough to disturb the bear."

Cooper's wide green eyes swung down to her. "You mean that thing has been tailing us all this time?"

He looked ready to lift his rifle again and as much as she wanted to defuse the situation and calm him down, she was too damned tired and shaken.

Wade scowled at Cooper. "If it has, it's your fault."

Cooper glared right back at him. "You've always had a problem with me. You blamed me for losing track of that cheating bastard's parents and now you want to blame me for a bear being on our tail."

Cheating bastard?

"Yeah, well, I'm not the one who let them slip away." Wade strode over to him and butted chests with Cooper, glowering down at him. "We had the woman where we wanted her. She would have talked if we had gotten our hands on her, but now she's in this godforsaken shithole wilderness and we're getting nowhere. You fucked us. We've got no leverage."

Skye stared up at them, her mind spinning. Had they wanted to use the woman's parents as leverage to make her talk? What was it the woman had done? Was the cheating bastard Knox or some other man?

"Wade," Karl barked and when Wade looked over his shoulder at him, Karl slid a pointed look at Skye. "I don't think this is something we need to discuss right now."

Because he didn't want her to know what was happening. What did it matter? If she didn't manage to get away from them, she was toast. She supposed that if she did get away from them and managed to reach the authorities, she would have a lot of dirt she could give them on Karl and his buddies.

"What happened to Patrick?" She looked from Karl to Wade and the grim looks on both of their faces told her that whatever had happened, it hadn't been pretty. She swallowed hard. "Is he...?"

Karl nodded.

Cooper sank to his backside on the log beside her, the butt of his rifle dropping to the dirt by his feet, and hung his hands between his knees as he stared into nothing. "Shit. Shit."

He scrubbed a hand over his face and growled in frustration as he shoved it into his hair and then smashed his fist into his leg.

"I'm going to kill that fucking bear," he snarled, tears shining in his eyes, and then his rage dropped away and he buried his face in his hand again, and whispered, "Shit."

Skye's brow furrowed as she looked at him, as polar emotions pulled her in two. She was relieved there was one less of them to stop her from escaping now, and one less of them for Knox to potentially deal with, but at the same time she felt bad that Patrick was dead and that Cooper was clearly hurting, grieving for his friend.

She placed a hand on his back and moved it in gentle circles, trying to comfort him, and felt like a bitch because part of her was hoping that bear would come back and take out another one of them for her or at least give her a chance to escape.

Cooper angled his head towards her and looked at her out of the corner of his eye. "You think it'll come back... like it's going to keep following us? It's going to kill us all, isn't it?"

"Shh." She kept rubbing his back and smiled for him. "It's long gone. You scared it away. It's not coming back."

That lie tasted bitter on her tongue as she kept on smiling, covering her fear, hiding how shaken she was as her mind kept replaying how that bear had charged towards them.

She couldn't shift the feeling that had come over her when she had locked gazes with it in the moment before Cooper had shot at it. It was ridiculous of her, but in that heart-stopping moment, she swore it had been charging towards her.

She swore it had looked desperate to reach her.

"We're moving. Now." Karl's barked words snapped her out of her thoughts.

She stared across the fire at him, her hand stilling against Cooper's back.

"It's safer by the fire though, right?" Cooper sounded uncertain as he glanced at her.

She shook her head and offered him an apologetic look when his face crumpled. His green eyes slid towards the woods, a flicker of fear in them that ran through her too.

"I know how you feel, Cooper." She kept her tone calm, gentle, trying to show him that she was on his side but convince him that he needed to listen to her at the same time. "The fire does look safe, but that bear killed Patrick and it's probably going to come back to—"

"Don't say it!" Cooper covered his ears and shook his head.

She wouldn't. Partly because she didn't want to upset him further and partly because she didn't want to think about the bear eating someone. It was rare for a bear to kill humans, but once a bear crossed that line and began predating on people, there was no going back for it. If the bear that had killed Patrick had developed a taste for humans, it would be coming back for more.

"It's not safe here." She gently stroked his back and leaned forwards so she could see his face when he looked down at his knees and curled over. "I'll keep my bear spray on hand and we'll make plenty of noise so the bear will stay away from us."

"We were making plenty of noise!" Cooper snapped and shoved upright, knocking her hand away. "We were talking and the bear still... it—"

"Oh, man the fuck up," Wade growled and grabbed the red pack and shoved it at Cooper. "Boss says we're moving, so we're moving. Got it? I am not hanging around here. You want to stay, go ahead."

He came to her and grabbed her arm before she could do anything, hauled her onto her feet and pushed her towards Karl.

"You can stay here alone," Wade spat at Cooper.

Cooper was quick to stand and slip his arms into the straps of his backpack. "Wait up."

"My pack and the bear spray." Skye pointed to it and regretted it when Wade was the one who retrieved it for her.

He came to her, that predator's smile in place as he twisted the backpack in his hands and held it up at shoulder height to her. She tried to take it but he drew it away from her, chastised her with a shake of his head. Nerves trickled through her veins and she had to pull down a breath as she mustered her courage. She scowled at him, making it clear she wasn't happy about what he was doing.

She doubted he cared.

She turned and slipped her arms into the straps of her pack, just about held her nerve when he lifted and smoothed the straps over her shoulders. When he brushed his fingers across the nape of her neck, she turned on him. Glared up into his eyes.

Skye backed away from him, keeping an eye on him. "My bear spray."

She held her hand out to him.

Karl stepped past her and took it from Wade. "I'll keep that."

She scowled at him, because hitting the men with a dose of the pepper spray and running had started sounding like a good plan. Instead of kicking up a fuss, she huffed and pivoted away from him, wrapped her arms around herself and walked a few feet towards the trees.

Her gaze caught on Patrick's rifle where it leaned against the log.

Wade was quick to come and snatch it up, to move it away from her reach by slinging it over his shoulder. He gave her a black look as he passed her, his dark eyebrows knitted hard and his lips compressed into a thin line. She didn't avert her gaze. She stared at him, letting him see that she had been thinking about grabbing the rifle and using it to blast a hole in him.

"Let's move." Karl jerked his head towards the trees.

Skye reached around and grabbed her flashlight from the side of her pack and clicked the button. She stepped up to Karl and motioned towards the forest with the beam.

"We should head around where the bear... Just in case." She started towards the left side of the clearing, away from the direction the bear had run and where Patrick had gone.

Karl followed her, his own flashlight cutting through the darkness.

"Let's get one thing straight, Miss Callaghan."

She slowly tensed as his deep voice rolled over her, a dark edge to it.

She glanced back at him and met his gaze.

His eyes were darker than ever.

"You even think about going for one of the guns... or leading us towards that bear... and our business relationship is going to reach an abrupt end."

The glacial look in his eyes told her what he meant by that.

One wrong move and he was going to kill her.

CHAPTER 10

Knox growled as he scrubbed snow over his hands and face, using it to clean the blood away. He paced between the trees, trying to work off some of his energy, some of his rage. On a vicious snarl, he turned and slammed his right fist into the thick trunk of a pine, stood there breathing hard and as still as a statue as fury blazed through him, refusing to abate.

Godsdammit.

He had been so close.

He drew his fist back and struck the tree again, close to roaring now, not feeling the pain that ricocheted up his arm or the cold as he stood naked in the forest.

Cooper had looked ready to piss himself and Knox had been sure he could take the male down, freeing Skye.

And then the Texan had pulled himself together and fired the rifle, giving Knox no choice but to retreat to avoid being shot. He was no use to Skye injured.

Gods. He scrubbed his aching hand down his face. He wasn't sure he was any use to her uninjured either. He should have been able to get her away from the males, should have kept his head and picked them off one by one as they panicked. Instead, he had made a beeline for her, leaving two men at his back who could have shot him, and coming dangerously close to being shot by the third because he had charged at him across open ground.

Knox gritted his teeth and growled through them. He flung his head back as frustration and rage got the better of him, every muscle in his body tensing as he unleashed another growl, this one loud enough that several roosting birds in the trees around him flew off into the night in panic.

He shoved away from the tree and paced again, breathing hard as he fought to calm himself. His bear side roared impatiently within him, a snarling and seething beast that urged him to find Skye. His female needed him. He couldn't. Not yet. He needed a few more minutes to rein his instincts back under control, to shut down the wild, reckless side of him that wanted to listen to his primal need to protect her. If he didn't get it under control, he was liable to do something stupid.

Like charging across open ground at an armed male.

He grimaced and paced harder, anger at how that male had treated Skye, stopping her from escaping and hurling her to the ground, replaced with anger directed at himself. He ran both of his hands through his hair and held his head as he walked back and forth, taking agitated strides between two fir trees. He should have held it together and stuck to the plan. Take out the solo male and then take advantage of the panic his death caused to divide and conquer his enemy.

Knox twisted and sank against a tree, the bark rough against his bare back. He exhaled hard. Cursed again.

He wasn't going to get another chance like that.

They were going to be more careful now.

He would have to find another way to get Skye away from them.

He pulled down a deep breath and then another, calming his racing heart, purging the fury that burned like fire in his blood. With each breath he managed, his mind slowly cleared and his bear side gradually settled as his thoughts turned from how he had failed Skye to how he was going to save her. He would save her.

There had to be a way.

One that wouldn't get them both killed.

He pushed away from the tree, strode to his clothes and tugged them on as he channelled his inner-Lowe. His twin would have been proud of him as he considered all the angles, ran through every scenario and tried to come up with a plan.

Tried being the operative word.

Knox finished tying his boots as his thoughts turned to his brother. He hoped Lowe and Cameo were both all right. He pushed to his feet and hurried towards the camp, his senses stretching out around him to locate Skye. Lowe had been injured when Knox had left him, part of the reason he had decided to be the one to deal with Karl and his men in order to protect Cameo. The thought of his brother out here, already wounded and trying to take down Karl turned his stomach and filled him with a burning need to deal with the male as soon as possible.

He knew Lowe.

As soon as he was able, Lowe would be coming to find him. His twin always had been a worrier.

Knox had this though.

He did.

He slowed his pace when he detected movement at the edges of his senses and eased forwards through the trees, using them as cover as he closed the distance between him and what he had felt. Skye's scent swirled around him, faint on the chilly night air but growing stronger as he approached the signatures he had picked up. It had to be her.

He slipped through the shadows, peering ahead of him into the darkness, relief swift to roll through him as he saw flashlights cutting through the gloom and Skye's scent grew stronger still. Shadowy figures appeared in the forest as he closed in on her and he eased back a few feet, until he could just about make them out. At this distance, they wouldn't be able to see him. His heightened vision revealed them to him without the need for a light. He tugged the hood of his black jacket up just in case anyway, covering his head, and tracked them.

They were moving slowly. Cautiously. Knox figured it wasn't only because of the darkness. All of them had looked tired before he had made the decision to attack Patrick and he had panicked them too. Regular fatigue and that caused by the drop in adrenaline was probably combining to make them all more tired than they had been before, slowing them down as their bodies and minds struggled to keep going.

Knox tailed them, still trying to come up with a plan. There had to be a way to get close enough to help Skye without blazing into the middle of the males and placing her in danger.

Or more danger than she was already in, anyway.

He scoped out the area they were passing through and relief was swift to sweep through him when he realised they had passed Black Ridge in the dark. His brother and his pride were safe then. Gods, that was a load off his shoulders. He just had to hope that Skye kept heading north towards the glacier, keeping his kin safe and giving him time to find a way to save her.

They suddenly stopped and Knox eased closer, curious as to why they had come to an abrupt halt. Cooper and Wade headed down the slope a little and then stopped, and turned slightly away from each other. Wade relieved himself against a tree while Cooper moved a few steps further from him and picked a bush.

Knox slid his gaze back towards Karl and Skye. She sank against a tree, facing towards him. Her sigh said what he could already feel in her. She was tired and worn down, on edge still.

The urge to go to her and hold her rushed through him again. He planted his right hand against the nearest tree and dug his emerging claws into the thick bark, anchoring himself to deny that need.

How different would things have been if he'd had the balls to see her again?

Seeing Lowe with Cameo had opened up the wound in his chest that had been festering for the last two years, poisoning his mind. Plenty of bear shifters found their mates in humans just like his brother had—just like Knox had—but it was different for him.

Or maybe it wasn't.

Maybe all bear males who were given a mortal fated female worried as much as he had over the last couple of years.

He knew how strong he was, had never been more aware of it than he was whenever he was near Skye, and he knew how rough he could be. He wasn't gentle like his brother. Lowe was level-headed and calm, rolled with things and didn't let them bother him. Knox wasn't like that. He hated to admit it, but he was quick to anger, had a temper that sparked at the slightest thing, and he was far more aggressive than his brother.

Lowe had been given all the good parts of their parents.

Knox had been given all the bad ones.

When his mood took a dark turn and anger seized hold of him, he had a bad tendency to lash out at others, both physically and verbally. The thought of Skye in the firing line of that side of him turned his stomach and had him wanting to take a step back from her.

She was too good for him.

He only had to look at her to know it.

He had seen her hold her own in a brawl and had seen her lay down the law with men twice her size, but she was kind and gentle too, had a big, warm heart that hadn't deserved to get a dent put in it by him.

Hell, maybe the fact she was too good for him wasn't the real reason he had never gone to see her.

Maybe he was just scared.

Scared that she wouldn't want him.

That she would never consent to step into his world and be his mate.

Maybe it had felt easier, and less painful, to keep his distance from her and carry on with his life.

Maybe he really needed to stop thinking *maybe* and admit to himself that it had been all those things and more that had kept him from going back to see her.

He wasn't strong. He wasn't brash and reckless. He wasn't himself. Not where she was concerned. She had a terrible way of stripping all of that away from him, leaving him weak and vulnerable, afraid to make a move because he feared she would never want him.

"Gods," he uttered and sank forwards, resting his head against his forearm as he pressed it to the trunk of the tree. "I'm pathetic."

Or maybe he was just a bear in love.

In love and terrified that if he admitted it to her, if he found the courage to take the leap, that things wouldn't turn out the way they had for Lowe.

Terrified that the happily forever after some secret part of him had been dreaming of from the moment he had set eyes on Skye would be denied him.

He would never know if he didn't try. Then again, did he want to know? Not when the greater part of him kept saying she would reject him. No. If he kept things as they were, then there was hope, a tiny seed of it that kept him going. If he didn't stride right up to her and tell her that he was crazy about her, that he loved her and wanted her as his mate, needed her to take an incredible leap and step into his world, then she couldn't reject him. He could carry on as he was, as a whole male, not the broken shell of one he would be if she turned him down.

Gods, Lowe would laugh at him if he were here. His brother would tell him to take the leap, to risk it all for the sake of love, and trust in fate. Destiny had made Skye for him, sure, but that didn't mean she would want a bond with him. That didn't mean she loved him.

Knox was starting to wish that just one of the thousand times he had wanted to tell Lowe about her and what he had done, that he had found the courage to go through with it.

Lowe had always been able to talk him down when he was spiralling, working himself tighter and tighter. He was sure his twin would have talked him down about Skye too, would have made him see that she was worth the risk and that love conquered all.

Or some bullshit like it.

His brother would have given him the courage he badly needed.

"How much further is it?" Karl's voice drifted through the waning darkness.

Skye eased away from the tree and peered up. Knox looked over his shoulder at the lightening sky too, trying to see what she was looking at, but the trees where he was were too closely packed together for him to make out anything.

As Knox looked back at Karl and caught him looking at the sky too, his features slowly hardening, he got a sinking feeling that she was running out of time. They would be on to her ruse soon and would know she was leading them nowhere.

"Maybe a mile more." She sounded bright as she glanced at Karl, as if she was relieved, but she didn't feel it to Knox. She felt scared. Suddenly more nervous than before. She gave Karl a half-smile.

"How do you know where this cabin is?" Karl frowned at her.

Cabin?

Knox's eyes widened as he remembered something and realised she wasn't leading the men nowhere—she was leading them somewhere. He had forgotten all about the old hunter's lodge up in the valley. He hadn't been up that way in years, not since the human male who had frequented it had stopped coming each summer. The cabin was small, hidden among the trees on this side of the valley, closer to the base of one of the largest peaks.

"This valley seems dead to me. I doubt anyone could live here." Wade rounded a tree to Skye's left and Knox wanted to growl when she jumped and twisted towards him, her hand coming up to her chest.

A chest the bastard dropped his gaze towards as he smiled at her.

Knox barely stopped himself from bursting from the trees to beat the crap out of the male, shut down that urge when Wade checked his assault rifle over.

"It's winter." Skye's tone was firm, had Knox smiling himself as he remembered her speaking to some of the men in the bar like that, subtly laying down the law and showing them who was boss. "In summer, it's a different picture. Hunters come here all the time."

They didn't.

The odd group of teenagers came up the valley, mostly young males trying to impress females, and the occasional serious hunter looking to bag himself a moose, but for the most part, the locals avoided the valley.

And with good reason.

Knox and his pride didn't exactly roll out the welcome mat for anyone who dared to set foot in their territory.

"The cabin belonged to an old friend of the family." Skye adjusted the strap of her dark green pack and sighed as a wistful look crossed her beautiful face. "He died a few years back, but his kids and grandkids use it now."

They didn't.

What she said explained why he hadn't seen the male for a while now, and had that feeling stirring inside him again, the one that made him deeply aware of how fragile humans were and how short their lives could be. Here he was pushing one hundred and thirty and with potentially a good few hundred years more ahead of him, and Skye had to be closing in on forty, was reaching the halfway point in her life.

Gods, he wanted to change that.

He wanted her to be his mate and share those centuries with him, looking as she was now, their lives bound together by an unbreakable bond.

Cooper rejoined the group and they started off again, heading towards the cabin.

It struck Knox that it was the opportunity he had been looking for. He took one last look at Skye to check that she was all right and then sprinted through the woods in the direction of the small lodge, trying to decide what he was going to do once he got there.

Continue stalking them.

Or make a move?

CHAPTER 11

Skye was bone-deep and soul-crushingly tired by the time they were close to the cabin, had never felt more depleted. It was as if her life had been draining from her with each step, leaving her feeling hollow inside, so tired she was dead on her feet.

God, she hoped she remembered where the cabin was and hadn't missed it or led Karl and his men on a wild goose chase. What if the family had torn it down? She had been lying through her back teeth to Karl and she feared she was about to pay her dues for it.

"How much further?" Cooper sounded as tired as she felt.

She flexed her numbed fingers and looked at the mountains that formed stark white jagged lines against the golden sky as the sun rose.

If she was remembering correctly, the cabin was just south of the pass between this valley and the next one, which meant it had to be a matter of feet from her now. The nearest mountain stood proud in front of the next one she could see, the sweeping slope of it that extended from the base of the high grey cliff beneath the peak cutting across the forest in the distance. That had to be the pass.

"We're close." She glanced back at Cooper and offered him a smile. "If no one is there, we can at least get warmed up and rest for a while."

Wade huffed.

She wanted to pick him up on it and the fact he was clearly going to side against her and Cooper and convince Karl to keep moving if no one was at the cabin, but she ignored him instead. For the last hour, he had been blissfully occupied with carrying out Karl's order to keep an eye on the forest, meaning he had left her alone.

Skye peered through the trees, trying to catch a glimpse of the cabin.

No one would be there. She knew that in her gut. They were miles from the coordinates Karl had given her for her GPS. The chances of them finding someone out at this remote cabin were extremely slim. Karl wasn't going to be happy, and she was going to have to calm him down and make him believe she was still useful to him.

Skye wasn't sure how the hell she was going to manage that.

She swallowed to wet her suddenly parched throat, and tried to banish the images of Karl putting a gun to her head and pulling the trigger that flooded her mind.

Ahead of her, the trees thinned and her heart leaped as she spotted the clearing and then a raised deck that had seen better days. Her nerves shot into overdrive, had her hands shaking as she started thinking of ways to calm Karl and stop him from killing her. She abruptly halted as the cabin came into view between two trees.

Smoke curled from the chimney.

Fear trickled through her for a different reason as guilt churned her stomach, making her feel sick. She had brought Karl and his men to this building and there was someone here. She had placed them in danger.

Karl unzipped his jacket enough that he could pull out his handgun. He signalled to Wade, gesturing for him to head to the left of the cabin, and silently directed Cooper to go to the right. She swallowed her racing heart as the two men moved stealthily through the trees to check out the cabin, studying every angle of it before both settled in a position where they had the small old wooden building that stood in the middle of the small clearing covered.

No escape for whoever was inside.

Skye took a step forwards, instinct pushing her to warn them they were in danger.

Karl seized her right wrist and pulled her back to him, causing her to bump into his chest. He snaked his left arm around the front of her throat, holding her at his mercy, and her brow furrowed as she stared at the cabin, as that urge to call out a warning continued to run through her. She tamped it down as Karl brought his other hand up, flashing the gun he was holding.

"What has this person done to deserve being hunted?" She tried to look over her shoulder at Karl as Wade and Cooper eased to their haunches and aimed their weapons at the cabin.

What if it was the woman they were looking for inside? What if she had led Karl right to her and now they were going to kill her? Oh God. She couldn't be responsible for an innocent person dying. She just couldn't. She had to find a way to alert them or get Karl to leave, giving them a chance to escape.

"They owe me a lot of money," Karl snarled into her ear. "I also think the bitch killed my men."

Skye jerked back against him as anger flared, hot and fierce in her veins. "The storm probably killed all of them, or the mountains... That bear—"

She cut herself off as the wooden door of the cabin creaked open and her gaze darted to it as Karl pulled her back behind a tree.

She couldn't believe her eyes.

"Knox?" she breathed as she stared at him where he stood in the doorway, his big body taking up most of the space.

He loomed like a malevolent shadow, his black trousers and boots, and his forest green and black checked fleece shirt that stretched tight over his broad chest, causing him to cut an imposing figure as he nursed a steaming mug and yawned.

"You know this man?" Karl breathed close to her ear and she nodded. Swallowed hard.

"Um... yeah. Knox... He was a regular at my bar for a while. I... I haven't seen him for a while though. I wondered where he'd gone." She dragged her gaze away from him and looked at the cabin.

Did he live here now?

"Prove you know him." Karl's grip on her tightened.

She scowled down at his arm. "How? All I can tell you is that he has blond hair beneath that black hat and blue eyes, and a scar... on his right shoulder."

She could almost feel Karl staring at the side of her face as she told him that, knew the look he would be giving her, and she regretted mentioning the scar and revealing she had seen Knox with his top off at the very least.

It seemed to be enough to make Karl believe her, because he put his gun away and zipped up his coat and signalled to Cooper and Wade, calling off his dogs. The two men stashed their guns, Wade placing his behind a bush and Cooper choosing to slip his behind some logs that stood near the old trunk of a tree that was being used as a chopping block, to the right of the side porch.

Karl released her and pushed her forwards, guiding her out from behind the tree. Her heart thundered, adrenaline rushing through her as she stepped into view.

Nerves turned to relief as Knox noticed her and smiled in a way that hit her as hard today as it had back when he had come to her bar.

He pulled his hat off and his smile widened, his baby blues twinkling with it. "Well, if it isn't Skye Callaghan. What are you doing so far from home?"

Beside her, Karl visibly relaxed and she wanted to hug Knox for making this so easy on her, proving to the man that they did know each other.

"These men are looking for people they know and they wanted a guide, so here I am." She shrugged and Knox's gaze slid from Karl to her, seared her with heat she hadn't felt in a long time, not since he had walked out of her life.

She refused to get caught up in him again.

But God, he looked so damned good as he stared at her, his dark blond hair damp and tousled and a fine dusting of stubble coating his square jaw. Intense blue eyes held her immobile, doing a better job of locking her in place than Karl's arm around her throat had.

"They came up here in this weather?" He lifted his mug and blew on the contents, his eyes never leaving hers.

Her heart did an irritating flip.

"They did. They sent GPS coordinates for a place up in this valley and that was the last we heard. Have you seen anyone?" Karl eyed him closely.

Knox just continued to stare at her, apparently unbothered by Karl or the two men who emerged from the trees to his left and right to flank him. "Nope. You want to come in and warm up? I can make more coffee. No milk though. No power up here and I haven't been able to get to town in months... not since the snow settled in."

How the hell could he be so relaxed? Either he was an amazing actor or he really didn't give a damn that three men he knew were armed and dangerous had him surrounded.

She wished she could be as calm as he was.

His blue eyes softened, a hint of worry warming them, and as much as she wanted to be angry with him, as much as she wanted to keep the shield around her heart in place and not let him in again, she couldn't stop herself from giving away everything she was feeling. She glanced at Karl and then dropped her gaze to her boots, fear getting the better of her.

Fear that she was going to get Knox killed.

She glanced at Knox, her brow furrowing as she thought about that, as it all played out in her head on repeat, tormenting her over and over again as the scenario changed each time but every time he ended up dead.

Knox's dark eyebrows knitted hard, narrowing his blue eyes, and his broad mouth flattened. All three men tensed as he took a hard step forwards and then swiftly closed the distance between her and him, not seeming to care that Karl stepped up beside her, moving slightly in front of her in a blatant attempt to make Knox back off again and show him who was in charge.

Knox just casually brushed him aside and stepped up to her, halting close to her, and God, he smelled good, exactly the way she remembered as his heat curled around her and she tilted her head back to meet his intense gaze.

"You look tired." His brow furrowed as he searched her eyes and she swore a war erupted in his, something savage battling the softer side of him, until he looked torn between touching her cheek and punching Karl. His voice dropped to a smooth, tingle-inducing whisper as he held her with his gaze. "Come inside. Get warmed up. Rest awhile. Let me take care of you."

Those six words hit her hard and she wanted to crumple, wanted to let herself go and stop clinging to the tattered shreds of her courage. She wanted to sink into his arms and let him be strong for her as everything that had happened rolled up on her and hit her hard now that she felt safe.

She nodded.

Knox slid a look at Karl, one that was all malevolence. "You're all welcome, of course. Maybe I can help you find who you're looking for. I know the valley well."

He didn't wait for Karl to respond.

He slid his arm around Skye's shoulders as he turned, the feel of his strong arm banded around her comforting her, increasing the urge to surrender to the pressing wave of everything that had happened and break down. She couldn't. Not yet. When she was safely away from Karl and he was no longer a threat to her, she would let herself break down. She would bawl her damned eyes out for once and just let all the fear, all the hurt, everything she had bottled up flow out of her.

Knox rubbed her arm through her jacket. "You all right?"

She quietly pulled down a breath and nodded. "Coffee sounds good."

He looked down at the mug and tilted it towards his broad chest as he muttered, "I'm not sure this qualifies as coffee."

He released her before she could ask what he meant by that and stepped up onto the deck, passing her. Karl caught her arm and she glanced over her shoulder at him, didn't need to be a mind reader to know what he was silently telling her as he glared at her. No sudden moves. She got the memo loud and clear. She wasn't going to try anything because she wasn't going to place Knox in danger. She couldn't.

She followed Knox into the cabin, Karl hot on her heels. It was small, but neat, and it looked lived in. Did Knox really live here? She studied him as he placed an old metal kettle on top of the ancient log burner, one that looked as if it had been the first to roll off the production line. He looked so relaxed that she actually began to believe he did live here.

But the place didn't smell very lived in.

It needed a good airing, was musty, and the more she looked around, the more she noticed odd things—like streaks of dust on the floorboards around the rickety wooden chairs, how worn the curtains were, and the fact that the springs on the small bed that stood in the far corner of the room were warped, pretty much completely gone.

She had the feeling she had been right and no one had been here since the old man had died, but Knox had come and tidied it in a hurry to give Karl and his men the impression someone did.

Wade lingered near the door. Cooper was polite enough to pick a chair to sit on. Karl stood sentinel near her, to her right, closer to the log burner.

Skye sat on the chair nearest Knox, diligently keeping her eyes off his backside as he leaned over the kettle. Her gaze roamed over him, up his arm to his face, and she passed the time by tracing his profile, something she had done more than once when they had been together. She had slipped into a sort of trance and spent a good fifteen minutes just staring at him like this once, back at her bar.

That had been the night one thing had led to another, and he had ended up breaking her damned heart.

His blue eyes slid to lock with hers, startling her out of her reverie.

"You're as beautiful as I remember." His whiskey-smooth voice warmed her, intoxicating her in that way it always had, and she drifted in the hazy feeling it induced in her for a moment.

And then snapped herself out of it and scowled at him.

"And you're as arrogant as I remember." She regretted that when the smile that had been curling his lips fell away and he averted his gaze.

He had never been arrogant. Not with her. He had been bold and brash, had been quick to get into fights and had spoken his mind to more than one man at the bar, acting just as arrogant as she had labelled him, but when it had come to her, he had been a different man.

Kind. Attentive. Sweet even.

Like she brought out another side of him.

One that, more than once, he had looked irritated about. She wasn't the only one who wore armour, hiding the softer side of herself behind a shield that stopped anyone from getting too close.

She wasn't the only one who was afraid of getting hurt.

But she was the one who had ended up hurt when he had walked out on her in the dead of night. She had learned her lesson when she had woken to find him gone, not even a note left for her.

Knox poured the coffee into several mugs and held the first one out to her, an apology in his eyes. She took it and busied herself in looking at it, trying to shut him and the guilt that squirmed in her stomach out. He had hurt her and he deserved to get the cold shoulder from her. Didn't he? Part of her wasn't sure. Part of her didn't want to punish him.

That part of her was pleased to see he was alive, was just happy to be close to him again. She wasn't sure what to make of that. She sipped her coffee as Knox handed mugs out to Karl and the others. Grimaced. Knox was right about it. It was hardly coffee. It tasted old and disgusting, and she didn't want to think about how out of date it was.

Either he had really bad taste in coffee or he didn't live here as she suspected.

Wind blew across the deck of the cabin, slamming the door shut, and Knox turned towards the window and stared out of it. Skye looked through the dirty panes too, watching the snow sweeping past.

"Weather is closing in. Might be another storm coming." Knox looked at her. "Maybe you ought to think about heading back down the valley before it cuts you all off."

"That's not going to happen. I need to find my friends. It's important." Karl set his mug down on the bench that acted as the kitchen counter.

"They're probably dead." Knox stared him down. "You need to get Skye off this mountain before the snow hits."

Darkness reigned in his eyes and she had the feeling that he was going to hit Karl if she didn't act fast.

"There was a bear attack," she blurted the first thing that came to her. "Karl is a bit upset because of it. The bear killed his friend."

Knox was quick to look away from everyone and stomp to the window. "A bear, huh? This deep in winter? Something must've pissed it off."

She didn't miss the way he looked at Wade, or the fact that hunger for violence that blazed in his eyes hadn't gone anywhere. Someone had definitely pissed Knox off, and she had the feeling it wasn't Karl who was top of his list. He looked like he was sizing Wade up for a coffin.

Because he had seen how Wade had acted around her?

Because he had seen how frightened she was of Wade?

She didn't want to think it might be that, even when her heart screamed that it was. Knox was trying to help her with her problem. He had led her to this place and she was sure he had a plan, a way of getting her safely away from Karl and his men. Knox cared about her.

She cursed. If he cared about her, then why the hell had he left while she had been sleeping? Why had he never tried to contact her? Never come to see her?

He looked at her as he turned and leaned against the wall near the window, his blue gaze steady and his air calm, but she could see the agitation in him, knew him well enough to spot that he was on edge around these men.

Or maybe it was being around her that had him so uneasy.

She wanted to ask him the thousand questions that had plagued her in the years since he had walked out on her, but she didn't want to lower her shield, and asking him would strip her armour from her and leave her exposed and vulnerable.

She forced herself to remain on topic instead. "I'm not sure what could have woken a bear at this time of year."

Knox grunted and shrugged. "Takes less than you think. Rowdy neighbours maybe? You been making lots of noise?"

"No." Karl's expression hardened as Knox slid him a look that called him a liar. "You're sure you haven't seen anyone or heard anything?"

Knox pulled a thoughtful face, pursing his lips as he frowned. He shook his head.

"Is there anywhere else our friends might have ended up?" Karl glanced at Wade.

The bastard meant to silently order his man to be ready to take Knox down. She shot to her feet, drawing Wade's focus to her instead, and froze. What now? Every man was looking at her. Her pulse thundered and she glanced at them all, and then smiled shakily.

"I thought I heard something. Just a bit jittery I guess." A lame excuse, but the best she could come up with on the spot.

"Nothing out there that's going to hurt you." Knox gave her a look that told her nothing in this cabin would hurt her either.

She wasn't worried about herself. She was worried about him. She kept facing him as she slid a look towards Karl, trying to tell him that the man was up to something.

Knox looked from her to Karl, darkness reigning in his eyes again. He rubbed his jaw, scratching his stubble close to the dimple in his chin. A dimple she distinctly remembered kissing once. It had made Knox smile, and then he had banded his arms around her, lifted her as if she weighed nothing and kissed her breathless.

She felt a little breathless all over again as she remembered the feel of his lips against hers, how intense his kiss had been, spreading warmth through her that had reached right down to her soul and set her on fire for him.

His gaze skimmed over her, darted back as he pulled in a breath. He stared at her, the hunger that surfaced in his gaze heating her, rousing that ache he had always stirred in her whenever he had looked at her like that—as if he wanted to devour her.

She swallowed hard.

Wade moved, stepping into the room, and she glanced at him. She didn't like the way he scowled at her and then at Knox, and looked as if he was contemplating hitting him or worse.

Knox casually looked across at Wade and stared him down until Wade looked away from him.

Unfortunately, that meant Wade was looking at her again. She kept her eyes locked on Knox, trying to shut Wade out, telling herself that Wade wouldn't try anything, not while they were in the cabin at least.

"There's a lodge up the valley, near the glacier." Knox dropped his hand to his side, his fingers curled into a fist, and then he folded his arms across his chest.

She had the distinct impression he had been contemplating punching Wade.

"There is?" Her eyebrows rose as she stared at Knox.

He nodded. "Private property. I'm not surprised you don't know about it. People who own it don't like trespassers. If your *friends* went up that way, they're probably dead."

It didn't deter Karl. "Do you have a map you can point it out on? I want to check it out."

"No. Don't need a map." Knox tapped his temple. "It's all up here. I know every inch of this valley."

Skye didn't like the way Karl looked at him, as if he was considering trading up, forcing Knox to guide him instead. Knox looked over his wide shoulder at the window.

"Weather is closing in fast. Last chance to get out of Dodge." His blue gaze slid back to Karl, as cold as the glacier he had mentioned.

"We'll be on our way then." Karl signalled to Wade and Cooper.

Relief swept through her and she silently thanked whatever higher power was watching over her as she moved to let Karl pass her. She was glad he had seen sense and they were going back to town.

Time slowed for her as Karl reached into his jacket and pulled out his gun, aiming it right at Knox.

"And you'll be leading the way to that lodge for me."

CHAPTER 12

Knox was like a coiled spring and the moment Karl made the mistake of drawing his weapon, pulling it out into the open, he reacted. He launched forwards faster than the humans could track him and batted the back of his right hand against Karl's, ripping a bellow from him. Knox caught the gun as it dropped and lunged for Skye's arm. He snatched hold of her and yanked her forwards with enough force that she yelped.

Knox pulled her to him as he twisted towards the door.

Ducked under the fist Wade swung at him and punched the male hard enough in his side that he heard ribs crack. Wade grunted and began to bend forwards, crumpling. Knox grabbed him and shoved him into the room, hurling him at Cooper and Karl. He didn't wait to see if Wade took them down.

He pushed Skye in front of him. She stumbled onto the deck and shrieked as a bullet tore through the doorframe just to her right. Godsdammit. More than just Karl had a handgun on him.

Knox saw red.

He growled and released her as he twisted at the waist and squeezed off a few rounds, nailed Cooper in the shoulder but the rest of his shots missed, hitting the doorframe and the log wall of the cabin. Cooper fell backwards but didn't miss a beat, fired his black pistol again. The bullet whizzed past Knox's head, dangerously close to hitting him. Too close.

The temptation to deal with the men here and now dissipated in an instant as he spotted Wade drawing another gun from beneath his jacket and sensed Skye growing more distant from him. Getting her to safety took priority.

He fired a few more rounds into the cabin, forcing all the males to duck and take cover, and kicked off as he spun on his heel to face the direction he had been heading before they had shot at Skye.

Only Skye wasn't there.

His head swung to his left and he growled again as he spotted her running into the woods in the direction she had come to reach the cabin. He caught up with her in a handful of strides and grabbed her arm, tugging her in the opposite direction, towards the glacier.

Knox gripped her hand in his left one and ran with her, weaving through the trees, forcing her to keep up with him. Her loud breaths cut through the thick silence as she struggled to match his pace and he wanted to growl again as he sensed her slowing, as he felt how tired she was and that she was close to stopping.

"I know you're tiring," he panted between breaths, his gaze zipping around ahead of them, charting a course that provided them with plenty of cover. "You can't rest now."

Behind them, gunshots rang out and she ducked. She stumbled into his side and he pulled his arm up, hauling her up with it, and yanked her against him. He turned with her, tugging her behind a tree, and plastered her to it, pinning and shielding her with his body. He peered around the broad trunk, breathing fast as his senses stretched out around them. Wind whipped past them, chilling his nape and his damp hair as it hurled snow at them, fat flakes that were growing more numerous as the seconds ticked past.

Knox inhaled a deep breath and looked over his shoulder towards the head of the valley. The storm would hit soon and it was going to hit hard. He didn't have much time to get Skye to the lodge.

He looked down at her, grew painfully aware of how he was pressed against her and how she was looking at him.

How warm and soft she was.

Gods, he hadn't been lying in the cabin. She was as beautiful as he remembered. She was older now, but if anything, she had only grown more beautiful. He touched her reddened cheek and frowned as he found she was freezing, the coldness of her skin against his shattering the moment and kicking him back into gear. He jammed the gun down the back of his pants and pulled her hood up for her, covering her hat and her braids, and lingered with his hand close to her face.

"Ready?" he breathed.

She nodded and he grabbed her hand and broke east, towards the mountain, hoping to throw the males off their trail. They hollered to each other in the distance, closing in fast. He kept running with Skye, his pace slower now, matching hers. The wind grew stronger, catching snow that had already fallen and swirling it up into the air. It gusted through the trees, causing the dark green canopy to sway and shed snow in places.

The storm hit as they reached an area of the forest where the trees were spread out, allowing the wind and the snow to gust down to the ground to batter him and Skye. The voices of the males grew more distant. Knox kept ploughing forwards, heading into the wind now. He grimaced as snow bit into his face and peered into it.

He brought his arm up and shielded his face with it as he ran, trying to keep his vision clear.

"How can you see where you're going?" Skye panted, sounding as tired as she felt on his senses.

Senses he was relying on more and more as the blizzard set in, stealing his sight from him.

"I know this valley like the back of my hand, remember?" He looked back at her, worry arrowing through him when he saw how tired she looked and how she was struggling to keep going.

"Where are you taking me?" She frowned and glanced around them, squinting as she tried to make out the forest.

"The lodge."

She missed a step. "Private property. Remember? Trespassers will be shot... or whatever you said."

"It is private property." He slowed a little for her, sure that the three males wouldn't be able to spot them in this storm. He couldn't see shit in it, so he doubted they could see more than a foot in front of their faces. "My property. Or at least it belongs to me and some friends."

Skye stumbled again.

Knox stopped, his heart thundering, blood pumping hard as he fought the fatigue running through him. The temperature was dropping fast and he needed to get Skye to shelter. He couldn't afford to rest. He couldn't afford to waste a single second.

"Here. Get on." He turned his back to her, offering it to her as he crouched slightly. He had thought it was better than carrying her princess style, but she still huffed. He looked back at her. "Get on, Skye. You're slowing me down and maybe one set of footprints in the snow will throw them off our trail."

His right eyebrow arched.

"In fact."

He went to the nearest fir, broke off a low branch that looked long enough, and strode back to her. She had huddled down into her jacket and tucked her hands beneath her arms, looked close to turning into a popsicle as she leaned into the wind and snow.

"Take this and hop on. You can cover our tracks behind us." He held the branch out to her, and she took it and stared at it. He turned his back to her again. "Now, get on."

She huffed. "No. If you want to cover our tracks, then we'll need to be walking anyway."

Knox grunted and looked to the forest canopy, seeking help there or maybe a sign from his ancestors, some way of keeping his temper in check as Skye pushed every damned button he had. "What is it with Grayson men and stubborn women?"

"Grayson?" she murmured, sounding intrigued.

So he might have never told her his last name. Another black mark against him probably.

"If you get on, I'll tell you my whole damned life story." He crouched again, making it easier for her and making it clear that he wasn't going to give up. He looked over his shoulder at her, his eyebrows drawing down. "Either you get on my back or I carry you. Choice is yours."

That had her rich brown eyes widening, revealing the flecks of gold that spotted the dark backdrop of her irises. Those eyes had bewitched him once and they still held power over him, made him want to stare into them forever to chart every spark of gold they contained and how they seemed to change with her mood or the lighting.

This time, she didn't put up a fight. She strode up to him, her eyes slowly narrowing, revealing she wasn't happy about being carried by him or his threat to hold her tucked against his chest, as if she was a fair damsel. She never had liked anyone making out she couldn't take care of herself.

She angled the branch away from him and clambered onto his back, and the moment he reached back and caught her under her thighs, he wanted to groan and his bear side instantly calmed. He straightened and started walking, tried to ignore the heat of her against his back or how her thighs were clamped tightly against his hips or how she was trying to throttle him with her right arm as she angled her chest away from him to sweep their tracks into the deepening snow.

He tried and failed.

The feel of her against him felt so good that it felt wrong. He shouldn't take pleasure from this, but by the gods, he did. All of his focus kept shifting to her as he quickly covered the uneven ground. He tried to keep it on his surroundings, not wanting to allow Karl and his men to get the jump on them, but it was impossible with her pressed so close to him.

And the scent of desire and spark of arousal he had felt in her back in the cabin stamped on his soul.

What had she been thinking about to rouse such a fierce passion and need in her?

Had she been thinking about him? About that night?

That little seed of hope that lived in his heart bloomed at the thought she still wanted him, grew stronger and made him braver.

"How much further is it?" She turned her head and her warm breath fanned his nape.

Knox growled low, every inch of him instantly hardening in response to the feel of her breath on his nape. Awareness shot through him, had his focus locking onto her, and the world narrowed down to only her. The part of him that had calmed when she had touched him grew restless again, his primal instincts firing to make him want to twist her in his arms and kiss her until she surrendered to him.

He squeezed his eyes shut and trudged onwards, attempting to shut down those instincts. Unfortunately, closing his eyes didn't help. He saw a flash of that moment in the cabin, when it had hit him that Skye was wearing her chestnut hair in twin braids that revealed the nape of her neck.

A nape he desperately wanted to sink his fangs into.

"Knox?" She leaned closer to him, her breasts pressing to his back, wreaking havoc on him together with how her jaw brushed his neck as she brought her mouth to his ear. "Did you hear me?"

He grunted, barely leashing another growl, aware that this close to him she would hear it over the noise of the wind as it shook the trees.

"Not much further," he bit out, cursed when he sounded terse. He softened his tone, which took a monumental effort when he was constantly on the verge of growling, wrestling the need to pin her against every damned tree they passed and kiss her. He should have kissed her when he'd had her pinned to that tree. "We'll be there soon."

He opened his eyes and focused on the route ahead of them, on protecting Skye. She went back to sweeping their tracks away, something a part of him knew was only going to delay Karl finding them.

The male would find them.

And Knox was fine with that.

He just needed time to get Skye settled in the lodge, get his fated female all safe and sound, out of danger.

And then he was going to deal with Karl and his men.

CHAPTER 13

It was pitch black by the time Knox finally slowed and began to walk up a rise in the woods where the trees were thin enough that she could see through the canopy in places. She wasn't sure how he could see where they were going. She could barely make out the trunks of the trees they passed and only those that were closest to them, within a few feet. Either he had really good night vision or he really did know this valley like the back of his hand as he had claimed.

Snow swirled around them again, growing heavier as they entered an area where the trees were even sparser.

She huddled against Knox's back, unashamedly stealing his heat. She had given up covering their tracks when the branch had felt as heavy as a lead weight in her hand, and the snow had been falling so thick and fast that it was covering their tracks for them. She had discarded the branch and opted to cuddle into Knox's broad back instead. He had responded by shifting his hands higher up her thighs and drawing her closer still, and had told her to keep her head down.

Skye had rested it against his spine, close to his nape, shielding herself from the snow and wind.

Snow and wind that had his fleece shirt soaked through. She was freezing, every muscle in her body stiff and her mind sluggish, and she was wearing a weatherproof coat designed for the frigid climate. She could only imagine how cold Knox was in only his shirt.

"We're here." Those words roused her from the sleep that beckoned her and she took hold of his shoulders and pulled herself up.

Her eyes widened.

The lodge wasn't small as she had expected.

It was a sprawling, single-storey log building that had a porch that ran around two sides of it—the front and an area to the right. Along that side, firewood had been stacked against a wall that capped it off at the far end, half-covered in a tarp. The middle of the lodge, where the door was, had a gable window above the sloping roof of the porch. Snow covered the entire roof and had built up in places around the raised deck.

Knox carried her up the steps to that deck and paused.

She realised he was waiting for her to get down. "I think I'm too stiff to move."

He chuckled warmly, heating her through. "You're fine just where you are. Hang on."

He reached up to the top of the doorframe, grabbed a key, and opened the door. The inside was even darker than it was outside, but Knox unerringly carried her to a couch, turned her back to it and eased down.

She dropped onto it and was thankful when Knox kept his back to her, giving her a moment to convince her legs to move. She slowly lowered them and moved them together, slumped on the couch in the darkness.

"I'll light a fire." Knox went to move.

She lunged upright and grabbed him, locking her hand tight around his wrist. "No. The men. They'll see the smoke."

Knox turned towards her and gently placed his hand over hers, and she wished she could see his face. His voice was soft, tender, a comfort to her as he said, "They'll see nothing in this storm, Skye, and I'm not about to let you freeze to death."

His hand brushed hers, fingers grazing her knuckles, working black magic on her that had her relaxing, the momentary burst of panic releasing her from its grip. She covered his hand with hers and held it a moment, not wanting him to let go and fearing that he might.

Two years she had been waiting to see him again and she still couldn't. She peered up into the darkness, wanting it gone so she could look into his eyes and see that everything was going to be all right.

So she could see in those same eyes that the moment they had shared had affected him as deeply as it had affected her.

She was dreaming now.

She released his hand and took her other one back, tucked both against her damp jacket as the warmth that had been slowly filling her fell away, leaving her frozen to her soul. Two years. Two long years and not once had he tried to contact her. If the moment they had shared had affected him as deeply as it had her, he wouldn't have walked out in the dead of night and never contacted her.

Knox lingered a moment and then he sighed and moved away from her. She busied herself with removing her boots, trying to shut him out and ignore what he was doing as he moved around only a few feet from her. A bright golden light flared and her head darted up, her eyes adjusting to the sudden burst of light. It chased over Knox's profile as he stared at the long match and then lowered it towards the grate of the fireplace. It didn't take long for the fire to catch and spread, brightening the room and revealing Knox to her.

His dark blond hair was slicked back, the wet strands shining in the firelight, and the handsome planes of his face had settled in a hard expression as he stared at the fire, shifting a log with the iron to allow the flames to spread beneath it.

A distance had grown between them since she had taken her hand back, one she knew was her fault. One she wasn't sure how to narrow down again. She hadn't meant to push him away, didn't want to be cold and bitter towards him, but she couldn't help it. Seeing him again after two years, having him act as if nothing had changed between them, as if those two years hadn't existed for him, was difficult for her. He had hurt her, and as much as she didn't want to be petty and punish him, part of her wanted him to hurt too. She wanted him to know the pain he had caused her.

"I'll... uh... I'll get the generator going." He stood and pivoted away from the fire, disappeared into a room off to her right, at the rear of the lodge, before she could say a word or stop him.

Skye unzipped her coat and looked at the L-shaped black couch, realised she couldn't dump the wet item on it and forced herself to stand. Her legs were still stiff as she walked to the front door and closed it. She lingered there, clutching her jacket in front of her as she stared out into the swirling storm. It was a whiteout. That gave her comfort, eased the part of her that feared Karl was going to appear at any moment.

Knox was right and the men wouldn't find the lodge in this storm in the dark. It would be a miracle if they found the lodge at all. They must have crossed the valley and covered a vast distance to reach this place. As far as she remembered, the glacier was a long way up the valley, almost twice the distance than the small hunter's cabin had been from the trailhead.

The lodge had to be further from the glacier than Knox had made it sound, because there was no way he could have covered that much ground in the middle of a snowstorm and in the dark too. He had been moving swiftly though, and now she was thinking about it, he hadn't needed a flashlight to illuminate the way for him. A hundred questions filled her mind.

They fled as a light flickered on, making her tense and her fingers tighten against her jacket. Something to her left beeped and she looked there. The light was one of three in the large modern kitchen area, suspended from a wooden crossbeam in the open vaulted ceiling. The other two in the black metal dome-shaped shades were out.

Skye hung her coat up near the door and checked her dark green sweater. It was damp at the hem where it had come loose from her black trousers, but she could live with that.

She hadn't expected such a well-appointed kitchen up here in the remote wilderness. There was a large stove in front of the window that overlooked the front porch and a double sink set into the wooden cabinets. Another window above it revealed the side porch she had seen. The worktop looked like solid black granite, which couldn't be right. It would weigh far too much for men to haul up here, even if they had a small four-by-four vehicle that could somehow traverse the forest to reach it. She didn't know of any road beyond the forestry track.

Maybe they had flown it in with a helicopter. Some of the bigger lodges in the valleys used local pilots to deliver building materials to them. It made a lot more sense to her than men carrying it all the way from the trailhead.

There was no way a group of men would be strong enough to haul it all that way, not even if there were half a dozen of them.

She moved to the wooden post at the start of the long row of cabinets that acted as an island and separated the kitchen from the living room and touched the counter. It was cold enough to be real stone.

A door beyond the L-shaped couch opened and she tensed, relaxed again as she spotted Knox dusting snow off his soaked fleece shirt.

"You'll catch your death in that." She regretted it the moment she said it, the second he looked at his shirt and then at her.

A wicked glint in his blue eyes.

He undid the top two buttons, reached over his back and pulled the shirt off in one fluid move, revealing his bare torso to her.

Oh God.

Her mouth dried out and she tried to avert her gaze, but it was glued to his body as he lowered his wet shirt to his side and stood there facing her, letting her stare. Tempting her. She swallowed hard, wanted to be angry with him for playing such a trump card, for trying to sway her and get her to lower her defences. Impossible. It was impossible to be angry while she was staring at perfection. There wasn't a man in this world who had a body like Knox's. It was cut from stone, honed by the finest sculptors, made to tempt women and set their biological clocks screaming at them.

Strong male. Competent male. Perfect breeding material.

He looked every bit a hunter, or perhaps a warrior, as he stood there staring at her, the broad slabs of his pectorals shifting with each breath.

She frowned.

Each increasingly unsteady breath.

Her gaze flicked up to his.

He looked away from her and strode to his right, disappearing beyond another door.

Had her staring rattled him? She had thought he would lap it up, that he would enjoy having her eyes on him, but she had the damnedest feeling that she had shaken him and made him nervous.

Which would be a first.

He had never been nervous around her before.

Was he waiting for her to give him hell?

If she did, he would deserve it, but right now she was too tired to get into a fight with him.

Skye moved to the fire and stood before it, staring at the flames, trying to enjoy the way they warmed her numbed toes and trying not to think about Knox warming her in a different way. She couldn't shake the feeling that something was wrong. The Knox she had known would have soaked up her attention, would have smiled in that cocksure way that had always made her roll her eyes. Something about him had changed.

An answer flickered through her mind and even though she tried not to, she latched onto it.

Did he have someone else?

Oh God. Was that why he hadn't contacted her? Was he married? Had he cheated on his wife with her? Her mind ran at a million miles per hour, racking up the questions, spiralling into a deep, dark rabbit hole of hurt.

"You okay?" Knox's voice coming from right beside her startled her and she whipped to face him, tripped on her foot and almost fell, but he snagged her wrist and kept her upright. His blue gaze leaped to his hand on her wrist and he was quick to release her. "Something on your mind?"

"No. Yes. What makes you say that?" She grimaced.

He frowned and eased closer, and God he smelled good. The black long-sleeved T-shirt he had pulled on did nothing to hide his muscles from her, seemed to emphasise every damned one.

"You look... I'm not sure. Maybe like you were chewing on a wasp. Or a bee." He glanced away from her, his face hardening, and grumbled under his breath, "Fucking bees."

She got the impression he really hated bees. "You allergic to them or something?"

He glanced at her and frowned, and then his brow relaxed. "No. Just hate how they stop me from getting their honey. Got a few bad experiences with bees under my belt."

"It's easier just to buy honey. I mean… who tries to take honey from a hive? Unless you keep bees?"

"Keep bees," he murmured thoughtfully, his eyes lighting up, as if that thought had never crossed his mind before but he liked the idea of it. "Honey tastes better fresh from the source."

They were getting off track. She tried to think of a way to get their conversation back on topic and then decided she didn't want to go back to thinking about the fact he might be married.

Her mouth had other ideas.

"Are you married?" she blurted and grimaced.

Smooth move.

He jerked backwards as if she had slapped him and frowned at her. "Married? Hell, no. I'm not married. Why are you asking me that—oh."

His eyebrows rose.

He swallowed hard.

"Skye…"

She shook her head and turned away from him, not wanting him to see that she was relieved to hear that he wasn't married. That relief was quick to dissipate when she considered he might have been married.

She pushed the words out. "When we… were you married then… or maybe you cheated on someone?"

"Where's all this coming from?" He reached for her and she moved a step forwards, stopping him from touching her.

He sighed and walked past her, ran a hand through his hair, tousling it as he went to the kitchen. He stopped near the island and pivoted to face her.

"I didn't cheat on anyone with you. Skye…" He huffed and frowned, drummed his fingers on the black stone counter, and then abruptly turned away from her again. "I'll get you a warm drink."

"I'll take a cold one." She held his gaze when he paused and looked back at her, surprise in his blue eyes. "I need something a little stiffer than coffee… and I'm also a little afraid you'll try to give me what you think passes for coffee. I'm not sure I can stomach another dose of whatever that was you gave me back at that cabin."

He half-smiled.

"I warned you it was awful." He shrugged and looked off to his left, out of the front window above the stove. "Lowe got all the cooking genes. He could have made even that out-of-date crap taste good."

This wasn't the first time she had heard him talk about his brother as if he was superior. It struck her that he measured himself against his twin and that deep inside, beyond all the armour he wore around his heart, he felt he was lacking. She was sure there were things he could do that Lowe couldn't. She walked over to him, drawn to him, needing to be close to him because despite his armour, she could see he was hurting and she wanted to know why.

She stopped close to him and angled her head up, her gaze colliding with his again. "About that drink."

He smiled easily this time.

"I have just the thing."

CHAPTER 14

Knox rounded the kitchen island, tugging the long sleeves of his black T-shirt up at the same time, revealing toned forearms that flexed and had those damned biological urges Skye was finding harder and harder to ignore growing stronger within her.

He stooped and opened a cupboard in the corner of the kitchen, near the sink, and when he turned and straightened, revealing the bottle he held, she smiled and shook her head.

Whiskey.

He grabbed two glasses from the cupboard above the one he had found the whiskey in and came back to her, choosing the other side of the island to her. He set the glasses down and pulled the stopper from the bottle.

She stared at the amber liquid as it sloshed into the glasses. It was strange having him being the one to serve her whiskey this time when she had done it for him so many times in the past. She lifted her head to tell him that and froze as her gaze caught on his face, as a feeling ran through her and had her thoughts shifting course.

Knox finished pouring two strong glasses of whiskey and looked up at her, still clutching the bottle. "What is it?"

"Nothing. I mean…" She stared at him, that feeling growing stronger. "It just hit me and… Well, I can't believe it's you… that you're really here… or that there are men after us. Everything just seems so… crazy. Surreal. Like a dream. Or a nightmare."

Knox set the whiskey down and offered his other hand to her, reaching across the black granite counter, his blue eyes earnest and open as he held her gaze. "I'm real enough."

She looked at his hand, tempted to take it. He had big hands. Strong, capable hands. They were as rugged as the rest of him, looked as if they could handle lifting logs and chopping wood with ease, or knocking a man out with a single punch, yet whenever he had touched her, they had been soft and gentle, applying just the right amount of pressure to make her burn for him.

Skye shifted her hand towards his. Stopped herself at the critical moment and reached for one of the glasses instead. She drew it to her and lowered her gaze to it, and Knox sighed and took his hand back, snagging the other glass on the way.

"This is..." Knox sighed again, making her want to look at him to see whether he was as conflicted as he sounded. "This is strange for me too. It's been a while since I last saw you, but it feels like only yesterday. Like the years just disappeared the moment I set eyes on you again."

She felt that too, but kept it to herself. She didn't feel it all the time. Sometimes, like now, she felt every day of those two years, the hurt she had felt in the weeks following their night together echoing inside her.

He glanced at her as she looked at him again, guilt flickering in his eyes before he looked at his whiskey.

"Don't worry about it." She tried to keep the bite from her tone but failed, couldn't hold back the hurt as it surged through her, the bitterness that had plagued her for months after he had left without a word. She called herself on that. The bitterness had lingered in her far longer than mere months. It had been festering inside her the entire time they had been apart. She had tried to forget him, but it had been impossible. Knox wasn't the kind of guy a woman could just let go. Or at least he was the kind of guy she couldn't just let go. "So you seduced me, left before I woke and I never heard from you again. There's absolutely no need for you to apologise to me."

"I did just save you." He frowned at her and regret crossed his features, softening them in an instant.

"That's debatable." She swirled her whiskey, lifted it and sipped it, but couldn't savour it as acid scoured her insides raw and her blood burned and chilled at the same time. The fear she had felt when she had been around Karl hadn't gone anywhere and she doubted it would while she knew he and his men were out there. She looked at Knox again, needing to hear him tell her that everything was going to be all right and needing him to confirm her suspicions. "They're going to come up here, aren't they? They're going to come for us."

He closed his eyes and nodded, and when he opened them again, steely resolve darkened his blue irises, that look in them all she needed to feel safe again. "When they get here, I'll be ready for them."

The part of her that couldn't let go of her hurt, that wanted to punish him, had her mouth moving before she could stop it. "Can you think of any reason why four armed men just happened to be heading up your valley? Maybe you slept with their sister or something and forgot to call her?"

He pulled a face.

"Ouch. Low blow." His handsome features smoothed, turning serious again. "They're after a woman. Cameo."

"Cameo, huh? Your girlfriend?" she bit out.

He frowned, the corners of his lips turning downwards as his head tilted slightly to his left, something she had noticed it always did when he wasn't impressed with someone. Fine, she was being difficult, but she couldn't stop herself even when she wanted things to be calm between them again.

"Cameo isn't my girlfriend." He twisted his glass in his fingers. "She's my brother's girlfriend."

She believed him as she sipped her whiskey again, enjoying it this time as her mood evened out and she shut down the part of her that kept wanting to lash out at Knox. Mostly because he looked close to answering some of her questions, ones that had been bothering her since she had found herself at a trailhead with four armed men.

"They mentioned a woman, and something about two men." She lowered her drink to rest on the counter.

"The two men are dead. Cameo is with my brother." Knox glanced at his whiskey, stared at it for so long she thought he might not say anything else, even when she could see the war in his eyes. He was debating whether to tell her something. What? It only made her want to know even more. He swigged his whiskey and huffed. "I wish you hadn't gotten involved in this."

Because it meant their paths had crossed again?

The look he gave her, one laced with pain and a hint of fear, told her that wasn't the reason. He was worried about her, afraid something might happen to her, and that touched her, softening her mood further, making it easier for her to ignore that part of her that wanted her to be angry with him.

"Cameo... she's a ranger and Karl is her ex. Apparently, when they were together, he was a decent man." Knox rubbed a hand over his damp blond hair and frowned as he shook his head slightly, his blue eyes telling her he found it hard to believe Karl had ever been a good man. "She left to become a ranger and her brother got caught up in some bad shit and Karl was apparently at the centre of it."

"What kind of bad shit?" She frowned and leaned closer, curious now. "Just what is it Karl and those men are involved in? Is it the mob?"

"The mob?" He looked as if he wanted to chuckle at that so she scowled at him. "He's a drug dealer. Some kind of boss or something. Cameo's brother skimmed money off his area's takings and Karl found out... and killed him... after he had told Karl that Cameo had the money."

"Fuck." It was the only response that sounded right in her mind. She had known Karl and the other men were bad news, but now that Knox had told her what they were and what they had done, it all felt so real. What the hell had she been thinking getting caught up in this? She should have listened to her gut. But at the time she had agreed to help Karl, her gut had been saying do it and she knew why. She sighed and muttered, "The shit I do for money."

"Money?" Knox leaned over the counter, resting his elbows on the black granite, closing the distance between them. His eyes searched hers as she lifted them to lock with his, that hint of worry they seemed to constantly hold when he was around her shining in them. "Why do you need money?"

She swallowed the rest of the whiskey, needing the numbing effect of it if she was going to talk about this, was going to open this wound and expose it to him.

She wasn't expecting him to kiss it better, but she needed to talk to someone about it. There were countless times she had come close to telling her staff, but every time she had lost her nerve, fearing that if she told them the bar was in trouble, they would leave to find another job rather than trying to help her save it. Deep in her heart she knew they wouldn't, knew they were her best friends and they always had her back, would help her through her troubles, but it didn't stop her from being scared.

Knox had that look in his eyes, one that made her feel he wanted to help her and needed to know what was wrong. He had looked at her like that so many times in the past, and every time she had opened up to him, and things had been better.

She wanted things to be better this time too.

Her gaze darted between his, a need welling inside her, pushing her to tell him.

To let him in.

"You can talk to me, Skye," he husked as his fair eyebrows furrowed, the tenderness in his deep voice and the look that crossed his handsome face warming her and giving her the strength she badly needed.

She knew she could talk to him. She always had been able to. He was a good listener, for her at least, and she had always found it so easy to tell him all her troubles. That hadn't changed. Something about him made her want to share the burden weighing heavily upon her heart. The same something that made her feel he was on her side as he waited, his gaze soft and steady, not rushing her but biding his time.

Because he knew she would tell him.

Just as she knew she could tell him anything and there wouldn't be any judgement. He wouldn't belittle her for coming dangerously close to failing at her dream. He would lift her up and help her, would support her and be the voice of comfort, one that would restore her strength and her faith that she could fix her problems.

"My bar." She sighed. "It's not doing so great right now. I can't lose it, Knox. That bar... it means everything to me."

"I know."

She shook her head, relief from finally talking to someone about this colliding with a desperate need to make him understand that her words hadn't been shallow, something anyone might say about something they loved.

He poured her another glass and topped his one up as she gathered her thoughts.

She smiled as he slid the glass back to her and she toyed with it.

"A few years after Billy died... He was my brother..." She wasn't sure she had ever talked about him to Knox. The surprise that shone in his eyes when she looked at him said she had neglected to mention Billy and she felt a little bad about it because he had told her about his family. "I don't really like to talk about him to others."

She wasn't sure why she felt the need to tell him that. Maybe it was the edge his gaze had, one that said he was a little irritated that he hadn't known she'd had a brother.

"I guess I should go further back." She swigged her whiskey and smiled tightly, trying to keep things light because she could already feel the hurt welling inside her, didn't want to let it drag her down to a point where she might do something terrible—like cry in front of Knox. "Might need another shot of this."

She waggled the glass at him, but his expression remained serious, his gaze searing her as he stared at her, as if he was willing her to talk and confess everything, to cleave a hole in her armour and let him see the other side.

The part of her she always kept hidden.

She sighed as he uncorked the bottle and poured more whiskey into her glass, watched the amber liquid flowing into it and swirling around. "We were both pretty reckless. Wild ones. We used to do everything together. Hiking. Kayaking. Rock-climbing. I wanted so badly to be like him. I pushed myself... hard sometimes. I did things that were way outside my comfort zone."

"Because you wanted your brother to see you in a positive light. You wanted him to love you as much as you loved him." He glanced down at his glass. "I get that."

She bet that he did. The urge to reach over and touch his hand was strong, the need to feel a physical connection to him flooding her with a desire to surrender to it this time. She needed the strength that would come from that connection, from feeling she wasn't alone.

She sipped her whiskey, hoping to find the courage she needed in it instead. "The day it happened... It was my birthday. I had just turned nineteen and Billy wanted to do something wild to celebrate. It was me, my now-ex and my brother. Billy suggested climbing and the weather was good for it, so I agreed. Shaw convinced him to swap an easier climb for one that was challenging even for a professional. Billy didn't look sure about it, and I knew in my gut he was trying to buy all of us an out by asking me to decide... If I wanted to climb it, then we would. God... I should have said no... but I didn't want to look like a scaredy cat in front of Shaw and I wanted Billy to see... It doesn't matter."

She stared at her drink as the events of that day played out in her mind as if they had just happened.

"We weren't that high off the ground when I slipped. Billy was above me with Shaw higher still, and I hadn't secured myself properly. The wire came loose and the whole of my weight pulled on Billy. It was a blur after that. I swung and hit a rock that jutted out, broke my damned leg. Billy tried to get to me and... I should have gone with my gut. It was the last thing I thought as Billy—" She swallowed hard and closed her eyes, not wanting to see him hitting the ground again, not wanting to watch him falling past her. "I was stupid. Reckless. I got my brother killed."

"You were a kid." Those words weren't a comfort to her.

She shook her head as her throat closed and tears burned the backs of her eyes. Her voice was tight as she said, "It felt as if my entire world had just fallen apart. Everything just took a backseat for me. My life got put on pause for a long time. I just sort of drifted. A few years after his death, my parents decided to move to the coast. They wanted me to go with them."

She swigged her whiskey, lost herself in watching it as she swirled it around and the amber liquid caught the solitary light above her.

"Dad tried to make me see that my dream of restoring the only local bar, one that had been closed for almost a decade, was only that—a dream. It was something I had wanted to do since me and Billy and our friends used to hang out in the old parking lot in the summer. One night I looked at it and then at everyone and thought how great it would be to have it as our place to hang out when we were all old enough... when we had grown up." Skye leaned back and looked at Knox, soaked up the sympathetic look he was giving her and how soft his gaze was—and how much he looked as if he wanted to come to her and hold her. She wanted that too. She wanted that with all her heart. "Dad did his best to convince me I would be better off going to the city and continuing my education."

"You didn't want to go?"

She shook her head.

"I didn't want to leave this place where we had grown up, where all my memories were. I thought..." She lowered her gaze again, couldn't look at him as she admitted this, in case he gave her a look that made her feel as crazy as she was going to sound. "I felt as if I would be abandoning Billy if I did. I felt that his spirit lived on here, in these mountains he loved so much. Life is tough here, but it's beautiful. It's home."

"What did you do?" He refilled his glass, proving her right about him. No judgement. No look that questioned her sanity. Just quiet, wonderful support that she needed so much right now. It was as if he could read her, was so attuned to her that he knew exactly what she needed from him. He glanced at her, a sombre edge to his sapphire gaze. "I had parents once. My dad was pushy. Always wanted me and Lowe to toe the line... something I wasn't good at. I was too much like Dad at that age. A little like you were. Reckless."

She was going to ask him about that later, was going to get his back story and learn all about him, but she needed to finish what she had started, needed to let him in and let him know her, all of her. Now that she had started, she couldn't stop. She wanted him to know things about her that she had never told anyone.

She wanted that connection to him.

"I went down to the creek that runs through the woods close to town and did a little soul-searching. Part of me knew my dad was right and that the bar was going to be a lot of work and might never be a success. I might be wasting my life on something that I could never pull off. Getting an education and a good job was the easier route. It was more secure. Less reckless." She tilted her glass back and forth. "I sat there for hours, going in circles. Do the sensible thing or run with my heart? I had almost settled on doing as my dad wanted."

"What made you change your mind?" Knox sipped his whiskey and leaned a little closer, had her gaze shifting to him and locking with his. The look in his eyes told her he really wanted to know and it told her something else too. He was glad she was opening up to him like this.

She was glad too. He had hurt her, but she didn't want there to be any bad blood between them. She wanted to move on and put the past behind her, and maybe see if she could have a second chance with him.

"This is going to sound crazy." She smiled, sure that he would think her insane when she told him what had helped her make her decision. She had never been into the spiritual, had never been one to see signs in anything, but that day had changed something fundamental inside her. "Promise you won't laugh."

The corners of his lips curled.

He reached for her hand and placed his over it. "I swear I won't."

She glanced down at their hands, at his big one that covered hers, absorbing his warmth and the softness of his touch, and how damned good it felt to have this physical connection to him. It calmed something inside her, soothed her in a way that moved her, had her aching to twist her hand beneath his and curl her fingers around to clutch it so he wouldn't let her go.

"A white moose strolled out of the woods on the other side of the creek and looked right at me. Just looked at me... calm as anything... and then it lowered its head to drink." She lifted her eyes to lock with his and struggled to hold his gaze, even though not a hint of a smile touched his lips. "I felt honoured by it. It honestly felt as if the land was showing me where I was meant to be. I felt as if it was my brother reaching out to me and it moved me to tears."

It was moving her to tears again, had them forming in her eyes despite how hard she tried to deny them.

Knox lifted his hand from hers and touched her cheek, his head canting to his left as he gazed softly at her. "It was a sign. Nature sent a spirit to guide you on your path and told you to remain here."

He looked oddly grateful for that. Because it meant they had met?

Part of her was grateful for that too. She had never felt a connection to anyone like the one she felt to Knox.

"Is that why your bar is called The Spirit Moose?" His eyes leaped between hers as his fingers lingered against her cheek, warming her skin and soothing her with that physical connection she craved with him, one that made the emotional one that came from telling him about her past feel even stronger.

Deeper.

She nodded. "I can't let it fail. When Karl slapped a thick wedge of money down on my bar top, I should have known there would be a catch... but all I saw was a way to save my bar."

He dropped his hand from her face and leaned back. "It seems really special to you."

"It is." She held his gaze as she thought about it, as she thought about her brother, and how she would feel if she lost the bar.

Hollow. Dead inside. Defeated. Her soul was in that bar. It was part of her. Vital to her.

"The place where I live, south of here, is like that for me." He swallowed his whiskey in one go and his eyes met hers again, their blue depths serious once more. "Special. I can't imagine what my life would be like without it. Without that place. It's my sanctuary."

That made her feel he really did understand her and knew how she felt about her bar. It made that connection she felt to him stronger still, making her feel closer to him, drawn to him.

"I'll help any way I can. I have some money." He looked down at his empty glass. Toyed with it. "I don't need it where I live. Maybe I can invest it in your bar?"

The soft warmth that had been filling her vanished in an instant, a prickly heat replacing it as the part of her that refused to let what he had done go rose back to the fore. Hurt welled again as she ran over his words and thought about his offer, part of her aware it was an olive branch he was offering while the rest felt it was a declaration of war.

The darker, hurt part of her won the battle.

"I'm worth your money, but not your time?" she bit out and huffed as she tightened her grip on her glass, looked down at it and considered drinking the two fingers of whiskey in one go. Because she wanted to let loose a little more or because she wanted to drown the hurt rolling through her?

"I didn't mean it like that." He reached for her and she stepped back, glared at him to keep him in place when he looked as if he might round the island to reach her.

The anger that had flared hot and hard in her veins rapidly gave way to the hurt, darkening her thoughts and weighing her down.

She slowly shook her head as she looked into his eyes. "Why didn't you call?"

He grabbed the bottle and she didn't miss that his hand was shaking as he poured whiskey into his glass, filling it almost to the brim. Great. She wasn't the only one who wanted to get drunk in order to make this whole thing easier to deal with. Now she was driving Knox to drink too.

He scrubbed a hand over his dark blond hair, mussing it, his muscles bunching beneath his tight T-shirt as he stopped with that hand against the back of his neck and heaved a sigh.

"I thought about calling you. I thought about it a lot. I had some things to work out... What happened between us... it... it..."

He was struggling, so Skye finished for him.

"It was nice, but it was just one night. I get it, Knox." She looked anywhere but at him, cursing the fact she was stuck in this lodge with him as he stared at her, as she couldn't hide how much that had hurt her.

Still hurt her.

"No," he barked. She tensed and her gaze leaped back to collide with his. He clenched his jaw. Swigged his whiskey. Ran his hand over his hair and looked ready to tear it out as his expression hardened and then softened again in an instant. His brow furrowed. "You don't get it. You can't possibly get it. What we shared... it... I got spooked."

"Spooked?" She frowned at him.

He downed his whiskey, poured another and drank that too. How the hell wasn't he drunk and passed out on the floor? He wasn't even slurring his words.

He sagged against the cupboard behind him on a long sigh, his gaze growing bleak, an edge of despair and hurt to it as he nursed his whiskey, holding it close to his chest. "I wasn't expecting you. I walked into your bar that day and saw you... and... I kept coming back because of you. I shouldn't have. We don't belong together, even if the universe says we do."

That was the whiskey talking.

Maybe he was more tipsy than she thought.

"Don't I get a say in things?" She stepped up to the counter and set her glass down, narrowing the distance between them as she searched his eyes.

He said nothing.

Skye took the bottle and topped her glass up. She stared at it as she thought about him and about what had happened, her mood levelling out again, the anger falling away and taking the hurt with it this time, leaving her calm.

"I wasn't expecting you either." She lifted her head and met his gaze again. "That night... everything just felt so right, Knox. As if we were meant to be together... As if... we had been made for each other."

He stared at her, looking as spooked as he had claimed to be that night as his blue eyes slowly widened.

She smiled down at her drink and let the past wash over her, recalled everything that had been good about it rather than focusing on the negatives. "I still can't hear that song without thinking of you. Every time it comes on the jukebox, I end up thinking about that night... About how we danced."

He blinked and then he was moving, setting his glass down and rounding the island to her side. He pulled something from his pocket. She frowned at it. A phone.

"I doubt you'll get service this high up in the valley." She tensed when he took her glass from her, his fingers brushing hers, and set that down on the black counter too.

He placed his phone down beside it.

She had wanted to ask him what he was doing, but as the first gentle strings of the song washed over her, she stilled and tingles swept down her arms and spine. The song they had danced to.

She stared at the screen of the phone and then at Knox. "You have this song on your cell?"

He glanced at it, a boyish edge to his expression that almost drew a smile from her. She had never seen Knox look awkward before, not like this.

He huffed and rubbed his neck, and wouldn't look at her. "You wouldn't believe how often I listen to it. You wouldn't believe how much I thought about you these last two years."

His gaze slid to lock with hers again, his eyes soft and warm, open to her.

She refused to tear up at that. That bitter part of her wanted to be angry with him again, but as he held his hand out to her, she couldn't resist him.

She slipped her hand into his and stepped into his arms as he opened them to her, settled her head against his chest and bit back a sigh as he held her. Her eyes slipped shut as they slow danced, as his heart drummed unsteadily against her ear, betraying his nerves. This song had become one of her all-time favourites because of him. It spoke to her in a way no other song had, seemed tied to him.

To them.

He leaned back slightly and she knew he wanted her to look at him, lifted her head and stared into his eyes. He took her breath away. There was such softness in his eyes—affection she wanted to believe.

"I'm sorry I didn't have the balls to call you." He feathered his fingers down her cheek and shook his head slightly as he swayed with her. His arm tightened around her back, tugging her closer to him, until there wasn't a molecule of air between them, and his gaze softened further as he angled his head towards her. His voice lowered, barely a whisper as he echoed the lyrics of the song. "You're all I want, Skye. You're all I need. I really mean that. You're everything to me and I know that—"

She pressed her finger to his lips, silencing him. That finger shook along with the rest of her as she stared into his eyes, as a need raced through her, slowly stealing control of her. She shouldn't do this. She knew that. She was only going to get her heart broken again.

Skye stepped back and broke free of his arms, her heart racing.

He sighed.

She went to the counter and grabbed her glass, swallowed the whiskey, needing the liquid courage.

And then she turned, walked right up to him, and stroked her hand down his broad chest.

His look went from one of defeat to one of uncertainty as his eyes darted between hers and he husked, "What are you doing?"

"This."

She tiptoed to kiss him.

He leaned his head back, stopping her, that nervous edge to his eyes growing as he frowned down at her. He wanted this. She could see it in his eyes, beyond the fear she didn't understand.

She wasn't going to let him stop her. If he was trying to be noble, he didn't need to be. If he was afraid of getting hurt, then he didn't have to worry—she would never hurt him. This wasn't about revenge. This was about putting their past behind them and picking up where they left off, because the feelings she had for Knox were too damn strong to be denied.

She loved him.

Skye lifted both of her hands to frame his face, her eyes darting between his now.

"I've been waiting two years for you, Knox... don't make me wait any longer."

He stared at her.

Growled like a beast just as she was contemplating making the first move.

And kissed the breath from her.

CHAPTER 15

Electric shivers danced down Skye's spine as Knox tugged her against him, his mouth claiming hers in a passionate kiss that lit her up inside and made everything come flooding back. God, she had dreamed of this kiss, but over the years they had been apart, she had somehow forgotten just how intense kissing him was. She sank into it, savouring it as his tongue teased the seam of her mouth and she opened for him.

He groaned and deepened the kiss, one hand falling to her backside to grip it as his other hand spread against her lower back, holding her in place.

As if she was going anywhere.

This was right where she wanted to be.

She had been through one hell of a wild ride over the last couple of days and she wasn't sure what the future would hold, but she wasn't going to squander this chance with Knox. She wasn't going to waste this moment. She had thought of Knox since the night he had left her, had wondered where he had gone and how things might have been between them if he hadn't walked out on her. She wasn't sure she would live to see what the future might hold for them, but she could damn well see what the present held for them.

Knox lifted her and turned with her, set her down on the counter and kept kissing her as his hands went to the hem of her jumper. She leaned back, breaking the kiss as the thought of him stripping her had her eager to do the same to him. She wanted to gaze at his body again and drink it all in just as she had earlier.

Skye grabbed the hem of his T-shirt and tugged it up, groaned as she revealed a strip of toned stomach and a treasure trail of hair that tracked down from the sensual dip of his navel, trying to distract her. She was determined to feast on the sight of him though, wouldn't rush this moment or skip ahead. She wanted this to be perfect.

He eased back as she slowly lifted his T-shirt, revealing him inch by delicious inch. Her breaths came faster as arousal soared, had her restless and itching to plant her hands against all that firm flesh and trace his muscles. When she reached halfway up his abs, he flexed, tearing a shocked little moan from her that she couldn't contain.

She scowled at him when he chuckled. Stilled. Damn, he was gorgeous when he grinned like that. It lit up his whole face, put a sparkle in his blue eyes and hit her hard in her heart. His smile slowly faded as she stared at him, a nervous edge entering his expression as he stared back at her, together with something else.

There was affection in his eyes as he looked at her, warmth that she had wanted to see in them, that made her feel she had been right all along and he did feel something for her.

Their moment in her bar had meant something to him.

His lips parted and he looked as if he wanted to apologise again so she dropped her hands to his hips, hooked her fingers into the waist of his black pants and tugged him to her. His apologetic looked shifted towards hungry as he lowered his gaze to her mouth, as she spread her thighs for him and pulled him between them.

He groaned as he dropped his head and captured her lips again, his hands claiming her hips, and she reached for his T-shirt, determined to strip it off him this time. She pushed the soft material up his body, brushing his muscles with her hands at the same time, eliciting another rumbling moan from him that had her desire spiralling higher, flooding her with heat and a need to kiss every inch of him.

She reached his chest and he shifted back again, raised his arms above his head and helped her remove his T-shirt.

Skye blew out a low whistle as she stared at him, appreciating every sculpted muscle of his torso as he stripped his top off and how his shoulders and arms flexed as he tossed it aside.

"Never met another man with a body like yours." She wriggled her fingers and went to touch him, but he caught her by her wrists, stopping her. She looked up at him, her gaze clashing with his.

"Another man?" His face darkened, jealousy flaring in his blue eyes and lacing his deep voice. "How many other men have you—forget I asked."

"None." She was quick to put it out there, because she wanted no secrets between them, no reason for this to go south and for things between them not to work out. "I haven't been with anyone since I was with you... You did a real number on my heart, Knox."

"I... I'm sorry. I didn't mean to hurt you." He raised his hand and palmed her cheek, his gaze earnest as his brow furrowed.

Skye placed her hand over his. "I didn't mean it like that. I meant you... kinda... might've... stolen it."

His expression changed in an instant, going from regret to something akin to pride or possibly relief. It was hard to tell because he slid his hand around her nape and hauled her to him, kissed her hard and pressed against her, bringing them into contact. He groaned as she wrapped her legs around his waist and pulled him closer still, so the evidence of his arousal pressed against her.

On a low growling sound, he grabbed her backside and rubbed between her legs, driving her mad with the friction. It wasn't enough.

She reached for the waist of his trousers, growing increasingly frustrated as she fumbled and tried to figure out how to get into them without breaking their kiss.

Knox pulled back, breathing hard, every muscle of his torso straining and distracting her. She stared at him, reeling a little from the sight of him, only half aware of what he was doing as he stripped her sweater and thermal top off and went to work on her black pants. Her fingers itched to stroke and trace every muscle, something she had wanted to do the last time they were together but things had been too frantic.

She didn't think she would get the chance this time either as Knox finally managed to get her trousers undone and tugged them down. Her backside hit cold granite, shocking her back to the world, and she looked down at herself. Her gaze caught on his fly and she couldn't stop herself from lunging for it, the hunger building inside her swift to steal control of her as Knox pulled her pants down to her knees. She wanted to growl when he moved back so he could push them down her shins, placing himself beyond her reach, but then he stole her breath by stripping them off and reaching for her breasts.

Her eyes rolled back as he palmed them, his large hands easily covering them, and her nipples hardened. The brush of his palms over them had shivers racing through her, cascading outwards from the centres of her breasts, and she moaned and tilted her head back, surrendering to him.

Knox dipped his head and kissed her chest, reached around her and unfastened her bra. The straps slipped down her arms and he loosed another growling sound that had a thrill chasing through her as he swooped on her breasts.

"Knox!" Her hands flew to his shoulders and she clutched them hard as he sucked her nipple, as he rolled it between his teeth and teased her to the point of pain.

She lifted her left hand to the back of his head, clutched his hair as he banded his arm around her and pulled her against him, holding her immobile as he swirled his tongue around her nipple. It was too much. Not nearly enough.

The fragile hold she had on her control was ripped from her when he palmed her backside with his other hand, as he eased it down to her hip and then around. She moaned and shuddered as he cupped her mound, as he stroked her through her panties, couldn't stop herself from working her hips and rubbing against his fingers. She needed more.

Knox yanked her panties down and she gasped. He swallowed it in a kiss as he made fast work of removing her underwear. His hands clamped down on her thighs and he eased them apart again, drove her wild as he slid his hands up the inside of her legs and brushed his thumbs upwards as he met her soft folds. He groaned and kissed her harder, stroked her again, slipping his thumb inside this time to tease her sensitive bead. She shuddered and moaned, her face screwing up as her mind raced forwards, imagining what came next, making her body hungry for it.

She couldn't take it.

She broke the kiss and seized his trousers, attacked his fly and won this time, getting the damn thing open. She moaned again as the two sides parted, revealing he wasn't wearing any underwear. She stared at the long hard shaft that jutted towards her from a nest of dark blond curls, felt in a daze as she reached for it and feathered her fingers over the blunt crown before stroking them downwards.

Knox grunted and gripped the counter beside her hips, his head dropping forwards as she explored him, as she teased him as he had teased her.

He grabbed her hand and pulled it away from him, seized her before she could protest, hooking his hands under her knees. He tugged her to meet him as he stepped forwards, pressed between her thighs and rubbed through her folds to torment her before he took hold of himself. He claimed her lips as he claimed her body, spearing her in one delicious thrust, seating himself to the hilt.

She moaned into his mouth and lost herself in how right it felt when he moved inside her, long slow strokes that had her soaring quickly towards release. She shuffled forwards, needing him deeper still, clutched his nape in one hand and his backside in the other, loving how it flexed with each pump of his hips. Heat swelled inside her as he kissed her, as he thrust into her, as he dug his fingers into her left buttock. She shivered and couldn't hold back the moan that burst from her as he pressed the fingers of his other hand into her nape.

A thousand thrills bolted through her, rippling down her spine, lighting her up inside as he held her nape in a hard grip and pumped her faster, harder.

Oh God.

He wasn't as intense as she remembered. He was far beyond that. Had her mind blanking and primal instincts stealing control. She surrendered to them, to the quest for pleasure, to the need to find release and pull him over the edge with her. She needed to feel him inside her, needed everything from him.

Knox dragged her right to the edge of the counter and curled his hips, taking her harder, his breaths sawing against her lips between each kiss. She reached for release, stretched for it as her body clamped around his and she rolled her hips. It hit her in a blinding wave of heat that seared her, had her crying into his mouth and jacking against him as tingles swept through her, as her body flexed and quivered.

He unleashed another feral sounding growl and gripped her harder, riding her release as he thrust deeper, faster still.

She moaned as he suddenly froze, buried to the hilt inside her, as deep as she could take him. He groaned against her lips as his cock kicked, as heat spilled inside her, and her body greedily clenched and unclenched him, wanting it all. Wanting more.

Knox pressed his forehead to hers, breathing as hard as she was, his grip on her so tight that she was sure he was going to leave bruises but she didn't care. She floated in his arms, lost in a hazy sea of bliss, unable to move as aftershocks rolled through her with each throb of his length.

A little moan of disapproval fell from her lips as he pulled out of her, but then he swept her into his arms, holding her like a princess, carrying her in the way he had threatened. Where? She tried to focus, but Knox was like a drug in her system, the pleasure he had given her still flowing through her, ebbing back and forth, keeping her hazy and aching all over for more.

He kissed her as he walked with her, a soft one that stirred warmth in her chest, increasing that feeling she had. He felt something for her. Something other than lust.

He settled her on a bed, stripped off and lay beside her, pulled her to him and held her. She sighed as she stroked his damp chest, slowly coming back to the world.

Fatigue rolled over her as Knox pulled the covers over her and held her to his side, as she used his chest as a pillow. She fought the lure of sleep, not wanting this moment to end, but she didn't have the energy to crack her eyes open, felt too incredibly sated to win against it.

Knox stroked her arm as she placed her leg over his. He gripped her under her knee and tugged her closer, so her front was pressed against his side, and then wrapped both arms around her.

She smiled and murmured, "Never had you pegged as a cuddler."

His soft chuckle warmed her and the way he kissed her hair stole her heart all over again.

"Don't tell anyone," he whispered, a teasing note in his voice. "My reputation will be ruined."

Skye snuggled into his side.

"I won't." She yawned and the tug of sleep grew too strong to resist. She slowly sank into it, feeling safe in Knox's arms, but a spark of panic shot through her and she couldn't stop herself from murmuring, "Don't go running off this time."

Knox kissed her hair again and held her closer still.

"I'll be here when you wake. I swear, I'm never leaving you again... There's no place else I want to be."

She smiled at that and let sleep claim her, sure that when she woke Knox would be there this time, and that the future she had always wanted for them was within her reach at last.

CHAPTER 16

The last two days had been something close to heaven. Passing the hours in the lodge with only Skye for company had him as near to happy as he had ever been. They had fallen into an easy rhythm, worked well together without having to communicate, as if they really had been made for each other. The only negative in a sea of positives was the shadow hanging over them.

He wanted to believe Karl wouldn't find this place, that the human had given up in the storm and turned back or had frozen to death. Which would be nice. Not so much the turning back part as the freezing to death part. He wasn't a fool though. He had given Karl a clear direction to head in and if the male had any survival instincts, he would have turned back to the small cabin and used it as a bunker to wait out the storm. As soon as it passed, the male and his lackeys would head out, striking north towards the glacier. It was visible from a ledge in the forest just a few hundred feet from the cabin.

Karl would know exactly where to come to find him and Skye.

Part of Knox was banking on that.

While he liked the idea of Karl giving up and leaving, he liked the idea of the male coming after him even more. He wanted to be sure the humans wouldn't return and that Cameo and Skye, would be safe from them, and that meant dealing with them.

"Do you think it's blowing over?" Skye looked back at him from the door of the lodge, where she had been for the last ten minutes, nursing a cup of coffee that had to be cold by now.

He abandoned his work of attempting to make a passable breakfast for the second day running and went to her. He meant to stop at the end of the island to lean against the thick wooden post there, but he couldn't stop himself from closing the distance between them down to nothing.

She smiled when he stepped up behind her and slid his arms around her, locking them over the front of her dark green woollen sweater, and even leaned back into him. A little sigh escaped her.

A sigh that echoed within him too, wanting out.

This was bliss.

If he could stay here with her and carry on like this, cut off from the world and pretending it didn't exist, that they didn't have responsibilities and a life waiting for them out there, he would be happy.

If he could continue burying his head in the snow and pretending that he would never have to come clean about what he was, then he would definitely be happy, but just like how Karl was a shadow hanging over them, that was a shadow hanging over him.

His only hope was that he could deal with Karl without an incident occurring that would give away what he was and then get Skye to Cameo. It was a solid plan, one he might have set in motion yesterday when a break in the storm had allowed him to get a decent signal on the two-way radio.

While Skye had been busy dealing with dinner, he had used the radio to contact Saint. He had been worried that Karl and his men weren't going to come up to the lodge and might end up there instead and had wanted to warn them. Once his alpha had been briefed on the fact there were three men remaining and all were armed and where he had left them, he had asked how things were at Black Ridge.

Knox had learned that Maverick and Rune had indeed returned to the Ridge, which was a comfort, until he thought about the fact that both bears wanted to come up to the lodge. Knox had talked them down, mostly because he worried about them meeting Skye. He hadn't told his alpha about her, wasn't really sure how to break it to him. Saint hadn't exactly taken it well when Lowe had brought Cameo, another human, to Black Ridge.

Bringing Skye there was liable to cause a ruckus with his alpha, but Knox needed her there.

He had the feeling that Maverick and Rune were going to ignore his warning to stay away from the lodge and come here, and he would be forced to deal with introducing her to his pride sooner than he wanted.

So, Knox had asked Saint to put Lowe on the line and clear everyone else out.

Apparently, Lowe had been hovering around Saint, twitchy and eager to get his turn on the radio, irritating their alpha. Saint had been all too happy to hand the mic over to Knox's twin.

Lowe had assured him the other bears were gone and had then gone on to tell him that Cameo was fine and his injuries were healing, which was a relief. Cameo had taken the fact Lowe was a bear shifter well, and that had given Knox hope that Skye might be the same, even when he knew there was a higher chance that his female would freak out and run. It was rare for a shifter to reveal what they were to a human and not get that reaction. It took a powerful sort of love, a deep and true sort, for a human in a relationship with a shifter to overcome what they were and accept it and the fact there were many different people in this world.

Archangel managed to fill their ranks quite nicely with the ones who discovered their lover was a shifter or a vampire or a fae and didn't take it well.

So Knox had decided to up his chances of Skye being the sort of female who could accept her male turned into a bear and lived longer than a human.

He had asked Lowe to speak with Cameo and convince her to talk to Skye when he got her to Black Ridge. If Cameo was the one who told her, maybe Skye would be able to take it all in without surrendering to the urge to run, or join a hunter organisation to eradicate his kind from the face of the planet.

It turned out Cameo had been there with Lowe and she had been quick to steal the mic from his brother and agree to help him.

Lowe had wanted to ask him a million questions about Skye and whether she was the reason for his two-year drought, and Knox had been quick to end the transmission.

Knox stared out at the storm, watching the snow falling, dancing in the breeze to flutter slowly to the ground. Skye was right. The storm was abating. The wind had dropped completely and visibility was improving.

"It's clearing up." He pressed a kiss to her cheek when he sensed that didn't please her. It worried her. He held her a little closer. "Nothing bad is going to happen to you, Skye."

She turned in his arms and looked up at him, her dark eyes soft, warm with affection that soothed his nerves and boosted his confidence that once she knew what he was, she wouldn't run. She wouldn't.

"What about you?" she whispered, her brow furrowing, and stroked her free hand down his chest, over his black-and-blue checked fleece shirt. "I have this horrible feeling something bad is going to happen to you."

He captured her hips and pulled her to him. "Nothing bad is going to happen to me either."

Words he meant but couldn't quite bring himself to believe.

She sighed and broke away from him, set her coffee down on the counter of the kitchen island and crossed the wooden floorboards to the window beyond the couch. She stood with her back to him, gazing out towards the glacier. She had been uneasy all morning, ever since they had finally rolled out of bed to see that the wind had dropped.

She wrapped her arms around herself, her fingers tugging at the fine material of her dark green sweater.

Knox tried not to stare at her nape, just as he had tried not to stare at it every second of every hour they had been at the lodge. The sight of it tormented him, had his bear side agitated and restless, filling him with a need to close the distance between them and feel her pressed against him. The feel of her soft body against his was enough to assuage his primal instincts as her male, took the edge off so he could resist his growing need to sink his fangs into that sweet, smooth skin to claim her as his mate and bind them together.

Skye hadn't helped by deciding to twist her hair into a knot this morning after she had freshened up.

Some part of him felt as if fate was testing him, seeing how far it could push him before he snapped. Fuck fate. He wasn't a slave to it. He was master of his body, not his instincts. He wouldn't surrender to the urges running through him, no matter how strong they grew. He would keep on resisting them until she was so in love with him that she couldn't leave him, even when she discovered he was a bear shifter.

And then he would keep on resisting the urge to bite her until she was ready, no matter how long that took.

He wanted to do things right, to be the sort of male she deserved, one who was worthy of her affection.

Even when part of him knew there would come a point where he wouldn't be able to resist the need to mate with her. He would snap. At some point, the urge would become too great, too pressing, and he would be too weak to resist it.

He ran his hand down his face. Prayed to the gods that she was ready to be his mate when that happened, because he didn't want to mess this all up, even when deep in his heart he knew he would. He had already messed up once with her. It would be all too easy to mess things up again and ruin this chance he had with her.

"You're thinking hard." She had turned to face him, her rich brown eyes soft with concern, laced with a hint of curiosity. Her rosy lips slowly curved into a teasing, almost wicked smile. "Thinking about me?"

She was fishing, and he was already hooked, was a goner where she was concerned. All she had to do was reel him in and promise to keep him rather than toss him back into the river, and he would stay by her side forever.

Would love her forever.

"Yeah." He scratched his nape, really tried not to think about how she would press her nails into it when they were making love, how she always gravitated to that spot. Did she notice how drawn to it she was? He pushed away from the door and rounded the island, sighed as he sank back against it. "Much as I love it here... alone with you... I think we should head back down the valley to town."

Because he wanted her safe, a long way from Karl and his men, far away when he tracked down the bastards and killed them. He didn't want her to see what he was going to do, even when he knew she was well aware of his plan to kill them and she didn't seem shocked or appalled by it.

She glanced over her shoulder at the window. The weather was clearing fast now and he could make out the mountain in the distance and parts of the glacier. The snow had stopped.

"I don't know." She shook her head and looked back at him, worry in her beguiling eyes now, fear that drew him to her. "What if Karl and the others have found this place and they're just biding their time... out there... waiting for us to emerge?"

If that was the case, he wanted her away from that damned window.

He crossed the room to her and pulled her away from it, into his arms, trying to act casual even when his heart was racing and his senses were stretching in all directions, hunting for a sign of life.

Knox turned with her and started backing her towards the kitchen, got distracted as her gaze collided with his, holding him fast. He wanted to growl whenever she looked at him like that, as if she was hungry for him, starving for her male to satisfy her. He swore he could feel how badly she needed him as his primal instincts fired, had him aching with a need to pleasure her, to give her what she wanted from him.

He groaned and dipped his head, captured her lips as he backed her against the island and planted his hands against the granite on either side of her hips, caging her with his body. She tasted like coffee, sweet and addictive, and he loved how she arched into his body as she feverishly sought more from him, attempting to steal control of the kiss.

He gripped her hips and tugged her hard against him, showing her who was in control, mastering her in a heartbeat. His pulse went wild as she surrendered to him on a husky moan, as she melted in his arms and pressed her hands to his chest. Gods, how this female owned him. All of him. She mastered him by submitting to him, made him a slave to her as she opened to him, as her tongue brushed his and her soft curves pressed against the hard planes of his body. If ever a female had been made for him, it was Skye.

Knox kissed her harder, deeper, aching for more of her as his body hummed with a need of her, with the first ripples of pleasure that swept through him that were a promise of more, of another intense moment with her that would leave him breathless again, reeling and even deeper in love with her.

He lifted her onto the counter, eager to take her on it just as he had the first night they had been here.

His senses sparked.

He stiffened as he detected movement outside.

The window behind him, where Skye had been standing only a minute ago, shattered, and she shrieked as the bullet tore through the wooden post at the end of the island to his right.

Missing him by less than an inch.

CHAPTER 17

Knox grabbed Skye, twisted with her and threw her onto the wooden floorboards. He covered her with his body, shielding her as his mind raced, as he breathed hard and tried to figure out what the hell to do. His canines elongated slightly as rage tried to get the better of him, pushing him to shift to protect Skye.

To protect his fated female.

The woman he loved.

He clamped his molars together and flattened his lips, refusing to let his bear side win. He couldn't shift. No matter how dire things got. In one-on-one combat, he would be able to take the humans, whether that was in his bear form or his human one, but they were heavily armed. Shifting into his bear form would put him at a disadvantage in this situation.

Plus, it would reveal what he was to Skye.

He couldn't afford for that to happen, not yet. He needed her to be wildly in love with him before they had that talk he dreaded, and he wanted it to be a talk. He didn't want to just suddenly shift in front of her and scare the living crap out of her, all ta-da! He needed to break things to her gently.

Another bullet ripped into the wooden post, lower now, and Skye shrieked again, her hands flying to cover her head. He covered it too, his head whipping to his right. He glared at the window. Where the hell had the sniper set up? There was a ridge a little way from the cabin, one that had good elevation, enough that the male could easily see into the building but not enough that he would be able to see them where they were on the floor.

That rifleman was making things tricky enough, but he could sense the other two closing in. If they got into the lodge and opened fire, there was a high chance that Skye would be caught in the crossfire. He couldn't let that happen. He needed to get her out of danger.

He eased back and grabbed her hand. "We're moving. Got it?"

She shook her head, her eyes wide, her face draining of colour. The fear he could feel in her beat in him too, but it wasn't fear of being shot or his life coming to an end here. It was fear of those things happening to her.

"We have to move, Skye," he bit out, harder now, some part of him aware that he had to take command, had to make her do as he wanted or she would just remain where she was, too terrified to move. "If I have to pick you up and run with you I will, but I'd rather you help me out here so we can keep low, below the field of vision of that sniper."

Her dark eyes widened further, the fear he could sense in her growing stronger as she stared at him. A split second later her features hardened, her jaw setting firm and her eyebrows pinching hard as a look of determination settled on her face. She nodded.

Apparently, she liked the thought of him exposing himself to a potential hail of bullets as much as he liked the thought of her doing that.

She took her hand from his and twisted onto her front, grabbed his hand again with her other one and took a deep breath. Her gaze leaped to his.

"You're going to be fine." He meant that. They weren't just empty words to placate her and keep her calm, convincing her to move. He meant every one of them. They came from his heart, from his fierce need to keep her safe. Whatever happened, he would make sure she made it through this.

He positioned himself beside her, between her and the window. Glanced at her again.

She nodded.

Knox kept low with her scrambling towards the couch, pulling her with him and using his body to shield her. Her harsh breaths scraped in his ears, the fear he could scent on her pushing him to his limit as he listened to her rapid heartbeat. He would keep her safe. No one was taking his fated one from him.

No one.

They reached the left side of the fireplace and the closed door there. He tugged Skye up and pressed her into the shadow of the deep doorframe, the chunky stone fireplace providing her some cover. The temptation to punch the door open was strong but he resisted it. This door had a lock. It would provide Skye with some protection. Probably only a few seconds protection, but still. It might be enough to save her life.

He reached for the door handle and quickly snatched his hand back as glass shattered. The bullet tore into the doorframe just beyond the handle.

"Fuck," he snarled.

"Are you hurt?" Skye sounded as terrified as she felt.

He was quick to shake his head, needing to alleviate some of that fear, keeping it at a manageable level. The last thing he needed was her going into a full meltdown. He doubted she would, because she was strong, knew how to handle herself, and she was a survivor, but he still wanted to keep her as calm as possible.

He drew down a breath and reached for the handle again, faster this time, managed to strike it and open the door before the bullet whizzed past him. He lunged into the bedroom, avoiding being hit, and turned to Skye, grabbed her hand and pulled her in with him.

He breathed a little easier with several walls between him and the sniper and no line of sight, but remained on guard, deeply aware that Karl and the other male were approaching from this side of the lodge.

Knox released her and went to the windows, tugged the drapes closed to provide them with some cover. He went back to Skye and took hold of her hand again, and gave it a gentle squeeze.

"We're moving again." He looked at her, sure she would refuse now that her fear levels were dropping. She felt safe in this room, but they couldn't remain here. He needed to reach his bedroom.

She surprised him by nodding, that determination flashing in her eyes again.

Knox kept low with her still, not trusting that the males wouldn't shoot out the windows, taking potshots in the hope the bullets would hit a mark. He banked right, heading for a door there. Skye kept up with him as they reached the corridor beyond it, as he took a left and led her along the hallway that allowed access to the other four bedrooms of the lodge.

His was the only one on the left side of the hallway. They reached the door and he opened it, pulled her inside and released her. He was thankful he had left the drapes that covered the only window in the room closed this morning. It meant he didn't have to close them, something that might have given their position away to the men.

"Wait here." He glanced at Skye and then hurried across the room to the double bed. He opened the drawer on the nightstand and pulled out the gun he had taken from Karl.

Checked it was loaded.

"Do you know how to use that thing?" Skye hissed.

"Sort of." He could pull the trigger and that was all there was to it, wasn't it?

"Sort of?" Her voice gained pitch and she scurried across the floor to him, a scowl darkening her features. She held her hand out to him expectantly. "Give me the gun. I've handled them at ranges before and know what to do if it seizes."

Hell no. There was no way he was giving her the gun. What kind of man would he look like then? He certainly wouldn't look great in her eyes, having to rely on a female to do his fighting for him. He could handle this.

He glanced at the gun. How hard could it be? Point. Shoot. He had done just that back in the woods.

"Is this a matter of male pride? I'm not going to think less of you because you let me have the gun." Skye rolled her fingers, a stern edge to her eyes now.

He pretended not to notice the hint to give her the gun or the fact she could apparently see straight through him.

"I've got this. Stay put and stay low." He moved to the door before she could protest and closed it behind him, lessening the chances of her seeing him fighting and the chances of the men finding her.

He flexed his fingers around the grip of the pistol. Frowned at it. Was he meant to hold it in both hands? He tried to think of how the people held guns in the movies and TV shows that Lowe loved downloading to his tablet whenever he was in town. He shrugged as he reached the wall that the fireplace backed onto and tried holding it in one hand, aiming it at the wall, and then tried again with two hands. Two hands felt better.

Rather than heading back through the bedroom to his right, he eased towards the open door at the end of the corridor to his left, one that led into the living room. He quickly peered around the door when he reached it and ducked behind cover. Probably a mistake. If the sniper had noticed him, he would have just given his position away. He grunted and flattened himself against the floor, crawling out in a marine commando way.

The front door off to his right burst open.

Knox's gaze swung that way.

Met Karl's.

Knox kicked off, hurling himself behind the L-shaped couch just as the male opened fire. Bullets ripped up the floorboards where he had been and he kept on moving as the second male, Wade, opened fire too. The assault rifle the bastard had made fast work of chewing up the black couch, whittling down Knox's cover and forcing him to move. He twisted and went to kick off again, his focus on the door of the larder directly opposite him, his thoughts on how the thick log wall would provide him with some cover.

A bullet ripped through the couch back and through his right arm, carving a hole in his biceps that felt like someone had just poured molten lava into his muscles and bones.

He grunted and moved the gun to his left hand, couldn't hold back the growl that rumbled up his throat as his canines elongated, as the agony and the rage and his need to protect Skye had the urge to shift surging through him. Thankfully, the pain kept it in check a little, but only a little.

Normally, pain forced bears and other shifters out of their animal forms, but right now he felt as if he could shift if he wanted it. Because Skye was in danger? His primal instinct to protect her was strong, had dense brown fur rippling over his body despite the fire that burned along his arm.

Knox shut it down and kicked off, hurled himself into the larder and collided with a lot of metal pots Lowe had stacked on the lower shelves, completely giving away his position. Not good. He ducked behind the thick log wall as bullets tore into the door and several thudded into the tins and packets of food stored in the room.

When the hail of bullets halted, a thick silence fell, interrupted only by the steady dripping of soup and other liquid from the punctured cans. Knox glanced around the door and fired off a few rounds. All of them missed, but he got better with the gun with each shot. The last one he fired before Wade finished reloading his assault rifle and unleashed hell on him had come close to nailing the bastard.

Knox growled at the thought of taking him down, both the bear and the man in him hungry for it to happen. The human would pay for the way he had acted around Skye, for that twisted flare of interest that had lit his eyes from time to time.

He curled into the corner as bullets shredded more of the food, causing an unholy mess that he knew his twin wasn't going to be happy about. If Knox survived this, he had one hell of a cleaning job ahead of him.

The gunfire halted again and Knox grinned and poked his head out. His turn. A bullet ripped into the doorframe right beside his head and he ducked back, his heart lodged in his throat. Fine. Not his turn. He growled and snarled as he realised he was pinned, that if he tried to look to aim, he was going to get his head blown off by the males who were waiting, biding their time.

A grunt sounded and Knox smelled blood. Not his.

He risked it, peeked out from behind his cover and really growled as he saw Wade and Karl both glaring at the door he had closed behind him and Skye, to the left of the fireplace. It was open. Fear sank icy claws into him as he looked at it, the relief that flowed through him when he didn't see Skye there only taking the edge off it.

Wade gripped the small knife lodged in his bicep and tugged it out, glared at it and then cast it aside. When the male turned towards the door, looking as if he was going to go after Skye, Knox lost it.

He growled as he broke cover, as his vision sharpened and locked onto Wade and he lifted his gun. He squeezed the trigger as soon as he had it lined up, wanted to roar as the bullet nailed Wade in the back of his head and blood sprayed across the wall in front of him.

He swung the gun to the left, aiming it at Karl.

Pulled the trigger as he grinned.

The gun clicked.

Just clicked.

No bullet.

No incredible looking and somewhat epic moment that would have Skye swooning.

"Shit," he bit out.

Karl smiled coldly and aimed his own pistol at Knox's head.

Skye came blazing out of the bedroom and leaped on Karl's back, throwing him off balance. He staggered backwards, his arm lifting as she locked hers around his throat and heaved. The bullet tore into the pitched ceiling. Karl regained his balance but kept moving backwards and slammed her into the wall.

Knox kicked off, vaulted the couch and hurled himself forwards into a roll as he hit the floorboards, snagging Wade's assault rifle on the way past. He stopped in a crouch and raised the gun, aiming it at Karl.

Froze.

He couldn't fire at Karl while Skye was still riding his back, clinging to him as the male slammed her into the wall again, clutching her arm now to keep her in place. He wouldn't shoot when he would be in danger of hitting her too.

"Shoot him," Skye gritted as Karl released her arm, reached over and managed to grab hold of her head. He bashed it against the logs behind her, ripping a pained grunt from her, but she didn't give up the fight. She battered him with her fists, pummelling his shoulder and the side of his head, and her dark eyes leaped to Knox. "Shoot!"

Not a chance in Hell of that happening.

He shook his head. He couldn't. She had to see that he couldn't.

She stilled and stared at him, affection in her eyes, as if he was the most wonderful male in the universe for not wanting to risk hurting her.

Then she screamed as Karl threw her, tossing her over his head. Her legs struck the kitchen island on the way down, ripping another grunt from her, and she disappeared from view. Karl lunged for her, and Knox knew the bastard was going to use her as a shield.

He squeezed the trigger before that could happen, his eyes widening as he unleashed a hail of bullets and fought to rein in the gun and get it under control. Several of the bullets tore into Karl and the male staggered back into the corner between the first kitchen cabinet and the wall of the lodge as blood exploded from the wounds.

Knox convinced himself to release the trigger as the male slumped, blood trickling from more than a dozen holes in his black jacket.

"Shit, this is more my style." He admired the gun as he approached the kitchen and grinned at Skye when she rolled her eyes at him.

She manoeuvred herself and sagged with her back against one of the cupboards of the kitchen island, breathing hard as her gaze drifted back to Karl. She paled a little. Looked as if she might vomit.

Knox lowered the gun and went to her. He set the gun down on the counter to his left and held his hand out to her, and breathed a sigh as she slipped hers into it. He hauled her onto her feet and into his arms, all the tension melting from him as he felt her pressing against him.

His senses sparked a warning.

He tightened his arms around Skye and rolled backwards, over the counter of the kitchen island, grunted as he landed on his injured arm on the other side of it as bullets pinged off the granite. Fuck. He had forgotten about Cooper.

Knox released Skye and pushed her behind him, gritting his teeth against the fierce sting as fresh blood bloomed on his arm. He felt her gaze on it, sensed her need to touch it, and glanced at her, silently telling her that he was fine.

His heart thundered as his mind raced, running through every scenario to find one where Skye and him would both make it out of this. Adrenaline surged, the need to shift quick to sweep through him. He couldn't. Skye would see. He looked up at the counter above him, weighing his options. If he could reach the gun, maybe he could take Cooper down too. He cursed himself for forgetting about him.

Before he could reach for it, Skye was on her feet and making a grab for it, completely exposing herself. She ducked back down, narrowly evading being shot as another bullet ricocheted off the counter, and he wanted to growl at her when he looked over his shoulder at her and found her checking the assault rifle.

The steely look in her eyes and the image she cut as she shouldered the weapon was both deeply erotic and incredibly terrifying.

He lunged for her.

She popped up and fired off a few rounds. No wild spray of bullets from her. Each shot was controlled. She ducked back down again before Cooper opened fire on her.

"Where the hell did you learn to fire an assault rifle like that?" he hissed. "At the range?"

"No." She shrugged. "Video games."

His eyes widened. He wanted to snatch the weapon from her, because shooting in a virtual environment with a controller was not the same as firing a weapon in real life as far as he was concerned. It might look like she knew what she was doing, was a seasoned pro, but what did he know about guns?

Enough to shove her backwards when Cooper opened fire. Bullets tore through the cabinets, emerging from the side they were on to embed into the floorboards.

Skye scrambled ahead of him, tucking the gun to her chest as he pushed her backside, making her head behind the couch.

"Provide some covering fire for me," he murmured quietly as he glared over his shoulder in the direction of Cooper, tracking the male with his senses.

Any moment now, the male was going to come out from behind the kitchen post and then it was game over.

The couch wouldn't be any match for the high-powered rifle the man wielded.

"Um." Skye rattled something.

"Um?" He didn't like the sound of that. He glanced at her and his gaze remained locked on her as she stared at the assault rifle and the thing that was in her hand. Magazine. The magazine.

She angled it towards him. "*Um.*"

No bullets.

"Fuck this shit," Knox snarled. "You're not dying here. We're not dying here."

If he had to shift into a bear to make sure that happened, he would do it.

He gauged where Cooper was with his senses, tracking the male as he eased deeper into the room.

"I know you're in here," Cooper called out.

Beside Knox, Skye froze, locking up tight. Her fear hit him hard.

He motioned to the other end of the couch and then to his left, trying to tell her to head around the couch near the windows. She nodded, got onto her hands and knees and hurried that way, following his instructions. He drew down a breath. Then another.

Skye hissed as she reached the area where broken glass littered the floorboards and the scent of her blood hit him hard, rousing a fierce need to growl and shift, to taste that blood by sinking his fangs into her nape.

Cooper swung in her direction.

Knox harnessed all of the aggression he felt as he thought about Cooper hurting Skye, as he thought about how in danger she was, and exploded from behind the couch.

A roar shattered the tense silence.

Not from him.

And then a huge cinnamon black bear came barrelling into the lodge on a collision course with Cooper's back.

CHAPTER 18

Skye couldn't believe her eyes as the enormous bear roared as it reared up and slammed its dinner-plate-sized front paws into Cooper's back, taking him down. The pain in her hand drifted to the back of her mind, replaced by terror as the beast snarled and bared fangs as it ripped into him with long claws, easily slicing through his blue jacket. Cooper's agonised screams and bellows rang in her ears and she tried to look away, but she couldn't. Her eyes remained glued to the poor man as the bear savaged him, brutally mauled him with claws and battered him with its huge paws.

Panic gripped her, the need to survive and to protect Knox blasting through her to make her move as Cooper went deathly still and silent. She scrambled for the gun he had dropped, her heart pounding so fast she felt dizzy, and her hands shook as she lifted it and aimed it at the bear. She shuffled away from it as it looked at her, tried to stand to move but her legs were like noodles beneath her.

The cinnamon bear roared and charged her.

Knox threw himself between her and the bear, his arms outstretched, as if that would be enough to block the bear and save her.

"Get out of the way!" she screamed, the sight on the rifle jittering around all over the place as she aimed at the bear. She couldn't get a clear shot with Knox in the way and she feared he was going to get himself killed if she didn't act fast. The bear was going to maul him the way it had Cooper.

"Back the fuck down!" Knox growled and she wasn't sure whether he was talking to her or to the bear as it advanced on him.

She locked up tight at the same time as the bear did.

The damned thing had to be at least five-hundred pounds, maybe more, and she had never seen a bear with so many scars. A particularly brutal one cut up the left side of its head, from just above its eye to over the crown of its head, close to its ear, and made it look as dangerous as she felt it was.

Why wasn't it attacking Knox?

She couldn't believe her eyes as it just stood there staring at him.

Not moving a muscle.

She really couldn't believe her eyes when a black-haired man jogged into the room, a little breathless, and his clear grey eyes landed on her and turned to steel as they dropped to the gun she desperately clutched in front of her.

He was big, rivalling Knox's size, packed with muscle that was clearly visible beneath his tight black woollen sweater and damp jeans. Another of Karl's men? She wasn't sure whether to swing the gun at him or keep it vaguely trained on the bear, wasn't sure of anything as she sat on her backside reeling and trying to figure out what the hell was happening.

"She isn't part of this." Knox eased back a step, moving closer to her, and slowly lowered his hands to his sides, but she didn't miss how he clenched his fists.

Neither did the black-haired man.

The sight of Knox preparing for a fight seemed to trigger something dark within him, had him flexing his fingers into fists too and angling his body, placing more of his weight on one foot. The grim planes of his face grew harder still, his eyes as cold as ice as he fixed them on Knox.

And then he suddenly relaxed, as if someone had flipped a switch in him, and did the craziest thing yet.

He walked right up to the moaning, restless bear and planted his hand between the beast's ears and rubbed its reddish-brown fur.

Skye stared at the animal, and then at the man, her gaze flicking back and forth between them as she tried to process what she was seeing. She had to be dreaming. Maybe the fear had become too much for her and she had passed out. This was all just some weird, crazy dream.

Knox turned to her and held his hands out with his palms facing her, approached her slowly as if he feared she was going to hurt him. She laughed at that, the sharp barked sound drawing the gaze of the black-haired man and the bear. Knox wasn't afraid of a bear or that man, but he was afraid of her. She laughed again. Couldn't stop herself.

She was definitely dreaming.

Or she had finally snapped.

Knox gently took hold of the barrel of the gun and then her hand. He eased her fingers open and took the gun from her, set it down on the floorboards beside him as he lowered himself into a crouch beside her. He brushed his fingers lightly over her palm and she sucked in a breath as the cut on her palm stung. She dragged her eyes away from the bear and the man, stared at Knox instead, into blue eyes that held more worry than she had ever seen in them.

He was scared.

Of the bear and the man?

Or something else?

Something deep inside her screamed that it wasn't the animal or the man he feared. It was her. He had that spooked look again, the one he'd had from time to time over the last few days they had been together in this cabin. The one that gave her the impression he was afraid he would never see her again.

Sometimes, she had caught him watching her, staring at her as if he was desperately trying to put her to memory, to capture every little thing about her. She had put it down to fear of losing her, that he was scared something would happen to her and she would be taken from him.

Now, she had the impression it wasn't fear of her dying that had put that look in his eyes.

It was fear of her leaving him by choice.

She looked between him and the bear and the man, going around and around.

"Hey. Don't worry about them." Knox smoothed his hand along her jaw. "Look at me."

Her gaze darted to him and away again, back to the bear. It huffed and she tensed, and the man gave it a chastising look.

"I know them. They're not going to hurt you, Skye." Knox applied gentle pressure to her cheek and she looked at him again, obeying his silent command.

She tried to keep her eyes on his, but it was impossible while there was a bear in the room. A huge bear with a bloodied face. A bear that was standing near Cooper's corpse. She swallowed the bile that rose into her throat and diligently kept her eyes away from the body. She tried not to think about Karl where he bent backwards over the kitchen counter either. Or Wade, who was laying face down beyond the black-haired man, his brains splattered up the wall, a gory backdrop that seemed to suit the man.

She swallowed hard, her entire body shaking as adrenaline and fear did a number on her.

"Look at me, Skye." Knox stroked his thumb over her cheek, his voice lowering, softening as he gazed at her. "Look at me."

Her eyes leaped to him and locked with his, and this time she managed to keep them on him.

"There's my girl. You're fine now. You're safe now. Maverick and Rune aren't going to hurt you." Knox smiled softly, his blue eyes brightening with it, but that edge of fear they held didn't go anywhere. "It's over, Skye. It's over."

He sank to his knees beside her, gathered her into his arms and held her, his cheek pressing to hers. She lifted her arms and wrapped them around him, needing to hold on to him, afraid too now as his words echoed in her mind and she heard a different meaning in them.

She didn't want to leave him. She didn't want him to leave her. And for some reason, she felt convinced that was going to happen, as if it was inevitable, already written in the cards for them.

They were going to be parted.

Again.

And it killed her.

Knox drew back and her gaze darted to the bear and the man again, her mind still struggling to process the fact he was petting the damned thing, calming it by degrees as he murmured things she couldn't hear to it. Was it a tame bear? One trained to attack on command maybe?

Knox palmed her upper arms, regaining her attention, and she looked at him, felt a little dazed as she gazed into his eyes and saw all the hurt in them, the fear, and what looked a hell of a lot like regret.

He looked as if he was breaking up with her.

She had seen that look on men's faces a few times, enough that she automatically braced herself for the 'it's not you, it's me' speech she felt sure was coming. Or maybe it would be the 'it was nice, but…' one.

He drew down a deep breath that shifted his chest beneath his shirt, stretching it tight across his broad shoulders, and exhaled hard.

She braced herself, tried to deny the tears that were already welling to the surface.

His eyes darted between hers, his dark blond eyebrows furrowing a little. "Skye, there's something I need to tell…"

Her eyes widened, his words lost on her as the bear behind him did the damnedest thing.

It rose onto its hind legs and transformed into a man.

A man!

A very naked man.

The huge brute stood even taller than the black-haired one, had glacial blue eyes that held no trace of emotion as he stared at her. The scar she had seen on the bear was there on him too, darting from his left temple up to the crown of his head, and there was a notch missing from his ear on that side. He looked like a fighter, was bigger than the other man, his muscles heavy and hard, making him look as if he would have enough power in one punch to knock a man out.

Or kill him.

Skye looked from him to the kitchen counter, to the half-empty bottle of whiskey that stood off to one side, close to the left wall.

She was either dreaming or really drunk. But she swore she hadn't touched a drop since the night they had arrived. Maybe it was the shock of everything making her see things.

"Fuck," Knox muttered and then glared over his shoulder at the two men. His jaw flexed and he gritted, "You two get to clean this mess up while I clean up your damned mess."

What did he mean by that? What mess had the men made? Her eyes slowly widened further as Knox pulled her onto her feet, as he helped her to the front door, shielding her gaze with his hand. Stopping her from looking at the bodies that littered the lodge.

Was he talking about Cooper? The man—bear—whatever he was had killed him, making a mess.

Or was he talking about the fact that same man—bear—whatever he was had transformed before her eyes?

Oh God.

She looked at Knox as they stepped out into the chilly air, a thought hitting her hard. The idea that had pinged into her head only grew clearer, gripped her more fiercely and made her want to put a voice behind the crazy notion, when the two men in the lodge behind her spoke to each other.

And one of them muttered, "How was I supposed to know Knox had a human with him?"

A *human*.

"Either I'm going crazy... or you can all..." She didn't want to say it. She wanted to just pretend none of this had happened. She wanted to go on with her life as it had been. Only she couldn't. There was no burying her head in the sand and forgetting what had happened and the things she had seen. She needed to know. "You can all turn into... bears?"

Something else hit her as Knox's face crumpled and he reached for her and then dropped his hand to his side and stepped back from her, a hurt look entering his eyes. That same look he'd had just minutes ago, when she had thought he was going to dump her.

"This is the reason you left that night." She closed the gap between them, unwilling to let him place any distance between them again, whether it was physically or emotionally. They had brought down their walls, shed their armour over the past few days and she was not going back to a hollow life without him. She wasn't going to let him give up on them. She wasn't going to run, even when he clearly expected her to, had braced himself for just that several times since that bear had barged into the lodge. She lunged for him and seized his hand, some desperate part of her pushing her to hold on to him, to make him see that she wouldn't let him go. She couldn't. She needed to know the truth though, sought it in his eyes. "This is why you left me, isn't it? Because you're like that man… those men… you can turn into a bear."

His throat worked on a hard swallow and she cursed the bleak look that entered his eyes, one that left her cold inside and had her feeling he was drawing away from her, desperately bringing up barriers to protect his heart.

Because he was convinced this was it for them.

Well, he was wrong about that.

He hadn't taken the time two years ago to find out whether she could live with the truth about him. He had convinced himself that she couldn't. He had given up before he had even tried. And that look in his eyes told her that he had spent every day of those two years building on that foundation, constructing and cementing his belief that this thing between them could never work.

He was wrong about that too.

"Prove it." She released his wrist and stepped back to give him room.

His blue gaze darted between hers and she knew what he wanted to ask her. He wanted to ask her not to do this, because he was scared. He was soul-deep terrified that she would run from him the second she saw him as a bear. He had feared that for two years.

Now, she was going to prove to him that he was wrong about her. Fear had made him weak. It had coloured his judgement and had made him ruin something that could have been amazing, tearing it all down before it had even got started.

When she realised he wasn't going to do it, she squared up to him again.

Looked him deep in the eye.

"You told me that we don't belong together even if the universe said we do." She searched his eyes, catching the barest hint of hope in them. Her brow furrowed and she reached her hands up, framed his face with her palms and kept his gaze on her. "Do you remember what I said?"

He nodded. Swallowed again.

But just as he had that night, he didn't say a word.

"I'm getting a say in this Knox, whether you like it or not... because this... this second chance we've been given... this is the universe telling us that we belong together. You can be scared. I am too... but I'm not the sort of woman who gives up when things get a little scary. When shit gets real, Skye Callaghan doesn't run, Knox. She fights." She brushed her thumbs across his cheeks and sighed. "When shit gets real for you, Knox Grayson... You're a fighter too."

She dropped her hand to his chest, placing it over his heart.

"I know you, Knox, better than you think I do. I know that deep in here, you want to fight. You want this as much as I do. I'm not running. Am I?" She smiled for him. "You expected me to run and I haven't. I won't. But I need to see the truth about you, Knox. I need to see it with my own eyes."

His face twisted and he looked away from her. He blew out his breath and his shoulders sagged, all the tension draining from him as he closed his eyes.

Nodded.

He stepped back from her and stripped his shirt off, followed by his black pants, stood before her naked and very distracting, and sighed again. The look he gave her offered her one last chance, an out she could take if she wanted it.

She gave him one in return. A look that demanded he get on with it.

Her mind struggled to compute what she was seeing as fur swept over his body, as it morphed into that of a bear, the whole process happening in only a few seconds. She stared at the big grizzly before her, and as the initial shock of seeing him transform from Knox into a bear slowly subsided, she realised something.

"You're the bear from the woods." She stared into his eyes, recalling how those same dark eyes had locked with hers that night. "You're the one who killed Patrick and then charged towards me. At the time I thought I was going crazy, because you looked so desperate to reach me."

Before she could find the courage to run her fingers through his fur, he shifted back, becoming Knox again. A terribly naked and tempting Knox.

"I *was* desperate," he whispered and reached for her, touched her cheek again and lowered his hand to her neck. He slid it around her nape and held it as he stared deep into her eyes and husked, "I was so scared you were going to get hurt. I wanted to get you out of there and I couldn't stop myself... When I'm in my animal form, instinct can take over, the logical human mind falling away as the animal one takes control. I couldn't stop myself from trying to reach you."

She cupped his cheek as she saw in his eyes how much he meant that, how badly he had needed to get her away from Karl and his men. He had managed it in the end, had brought her through this whole ordeal unscathed.

But altered.

Her entire world was different now. She was different. But in a good way. She felt that deep in her heart, in her soul. From here on out, things were going to be better, brighter. They were going to be everything she had wanted for the last few years.

"I know we're too different, Skye. I know I don't belong in your world." Those words leaving his lips left her cold and she wanted to curse him for trying to bring up that wall between them, for letting fear get the better of him and ruining her moment.

She was having that future she wanted with him, whether he liked it or not. All she had to do was come up with the perfect counter-argument and he would crumble. She could see it in his eyes. He was reaching, desperately trying to get her to break down his defences and show him that she wanted him, that she felt something for him, and that the fact he could turn into a bear didn't change a damned thing.

Which sounded crazy as she thought it.

But she always had been a little crazy.

"It seems like the same world to me." She looked around at her and took a deep breath, savouring the cold air, the crisp scent of snow and Knox, and how bright everything was. How beautiful. "Same small town. Same wild valleys."

She shifted her gaze to him.

"Same Knox. Same Skye. All I see before me is the man I fell for... an idiot who walked out on me. Don't walk out on me again."

He stared at her. "Fell for?"

And there it was.

That spark of hope, of resolve. The fighter coming to the fore now that his fears had been silenced.

"It was never a one-night stand to me, Knox. It was never too much whiskey and too many lonely nights." She sighed. "I fell for you a long time before that night."

His blue eyes softened and warmed, shining with affection. "It was never like that for me either. I think I fell for you the second I set eyes on you."

She smiled at that, warmed from head to toe, not feeling the chill of the winter air as she bathed in the heat of the look he was giving her. She wanted to kiss him too.

His gaze dropped to her lips, growing hooded as he gently pulled her towards him.

Skye wrapped her arms around his neck, embracing her future, as crazy as it might be, and kissed him.

CHAPTER 19

Knox put the black truck into park and slipped from the cab. He squinted and covered his eyes as his boots hit the sidewalk, tilted his head back and gazed at the endless blue sky. Around him, insects buzzed, busy as the chill of winter finally gave way to the warmth of late spring. He slammed the door of his old, beaten-up truck and tugged the long sleeves of his black T-shirt up his forearms. The temperature in town was warmer than it was in the valley still, the added altitude keeping Black Ridge cooler. He had ditched his shirt already and was regretting wearing a long sleeve now.

The people coming and going along the main street of the small town paid him no heed, went about their day as if there wasn't a bear shifter standing among them, just the way he liked it. He hated it when people stared. It always put him on edge and made him worry that they knew what he was.

He locked the truck, slipped the keys into the pocket of his black jeans, and turned slowly to face the direction of The Spirit Moose. The bar was set back on an open lot, with space in front of it for tables and chairs, and a car park off to the right. It looked like an old lodge, with thick posts and beams that were dark with age and a carved wooden moose head hanging on the log wall above the door. The pitched roof overhung on one side, providing shelter for a seating area on a large deck, and at the gable too.

Outside, several of the tables were already busy with patrons enjoying a cold glass of something in the warm sunshine.

Another busy day for the bar.

He could already see how happy Skye would be, how there would be a bounce in her step and a smile on her face as she worked hard.

It made him smile too.

Several months had passed since she had discovered what he was and she had taken it all in her stride. When he had returned her to town once he was sure she was over the shock of everything that had happened, she had told him to come by that weekend to pick her up for their first date.

They had been dating ever since, with him always coming to her bar and spending a few hours talking to her whenever she had a moment and watching over her to make sure none of the local males got ideas about hitting on his female. Apparently, he was an excellent deterrent. Not a single male dared to even look at her for longer than it took to order a drink, and many of them didn't even manage that. Most of them stared at their hands or the bar counter while he glared at them.

The bear side of him wanted Skye far away from all the unmated males who frequented her bar.

The human side of him knew this was her home. It always would be, no matter how things turned out for them.

The Spirit Moose was important to her, a part of her life she couldn't leave behind and he would never expect her to do such a thing. It was part of the reason he had continued living at Black Ridge while she had remained living in town at her bar.

The rest of that reason was the fact that if he spent more than a day or two around her, his primal instincts had him dangerously close to claiming her, the need to sink his fangs into her nape and bind them as mates becoming unbearable.

Whenever that happened, he made his excuses and left.

Five weeks ago, Skye had called him on it, demanding to know why he insisted on leaving her at times—sometimes when things between them were just getting damned good.

Seeing in her eyes that she believed he was losing interest in her, feeling the fear in her and the hurt, had helped him find his balls.

He had confessed that she was his fated one and what that meant, part of him expecting her to end things or finally change her mind about them.

Not his Skye. She was right. She didn't run when things got scary. She fought.

She had told him that when she was ready, they could be mates.

Knox had been utterly blown away by that.

For two years, he had been convinced she would never be his mate, and now he felt agonisingly close to having her as just that. Gods, he wanted it. He wanted it so badly he'd had to leave the second she had told him that and had struggled to stay away from her for a week, giving himself enough time to cool down.

It was getting harder and harder for him to keep his head around her now.

As much as he loved visiting her, as eager as he was to see her, he dreaded it too.

He strode towards the bar, paused as the wooden troughs that were a recent addition caught his eye. They lined the front edge of the deck and were spaced at intervals around the seating on the asphalt too, forming a sort of perimeter. Someone had planted flowers of different shapes and sizes in them, providing a sprinkling of colour that seemed to herald that summer was here and brightened everything.

Knox stole one of the pink flowers, one that resembled a large daisy with a thick stem, and hurried up the steps onto the deck. He eased the door open, wanting to surprise Skye since he wasn't due to be here for hours yet. He had been too restless at the Ridge, eager to see her, and Lowe had told him to get the hell out of his cabin and stop bugging him and Cameo.

So Knox had come to town early.

To surprise his female.

Only the damned door creaked and gave him away.

Skye dazzled him with a smile as she lifted her head and looked towards the door, pausing halfway through wiping down one of the wooden tables. Her rich chocolate eyes lit up as they landed on him. She wiped her hands on a towel and jammed it into her dark blue jeans as she hurried to him, her smile infectious, causing his lips to curve into a grin.

He caught her as she hurled herself at him, lifted her and kissed her as she draped her arms around his neck. The kiss was over too soon, ended just as he was getting into it.

"Hey there, handsome." She gripped his shoulders, smiling down into his eyes as he held her aloft. "I'm guessing you missed me so much you just couldn't stay away another second."

Gods, this female knew him too well. Saw straight through him.

"Guessing you missed me too, judging by that welcome." He eased her down to him and captured her lips again.

He wanted to groan as her lips brushed his, sending heat rolling through him, but was deeply aware they had company.

Skye broke the kiss again and pushed back. Her dark eyes fell to the flower he gripped in his other hand and darted back to meet his.

"That for me?" Her eyebrows rose, warmth flooding her irises as her smile widened a little.

He chuckled. "It was for Lowe, but I suppose I can let you have it."

She rolled her eyes at him and snatched the flower, smiled at it and then frowned. Her eyes lifted to lock with his again.

"Is this from my planters?" She sighed and tapped him on the forehead with the flower when he grinned at her, not feeling even a trace of regret over his actions. She pulled a face at him, but there was no real anger in it. "I just planted those."

He released her when she pushed against him, letting her drop to her feet.

"How is Lowe?" She twirled the flower in her fingers. "And Cameo, and Holly?"

"They're all good. The others are too." He added that because she never asked about Rune or Maverick, had a tendency to avoid them as much as possible whenever she came to the Ridge. He knew Rune had scared her though so he could understand that.

The two bears had been keeping to themselves recently anyway.

"There's a get-together tonight." He gave her a hopeful look, because Saint expected him to be there and he couldn't disobey his alpha, even when he wanted to be here with Skye, didn't want to miss one of their dates.

She rubbed her neck and rolled her head, grimacing as her eyes closed.

She pouted as she looked at him. "I want to go too. I've been working flat out this week."

Knox rubbed her shoulders through her worn black Guns N' Roses T-shirt, growing aware of something.

She had twisted her dark hair up into a knot at the back of her head, exposing her nape in a way that felt intentional to him as he gazed at it. He shook that off. It was warm today and she had been busy, had probably tied her hair away from her neck because she was hot and sticky, and had wanted to cool down, not because she was trying to get his eyes on her nape.

Still, he couldn't stop staring at her bare neck as he murmured, "I'd like you to come. Everyone would love to see you again."

Stacy, the mousy-haired female behind the bar, hollered, "Go! I'll cover tonight with Jon."

Skye looked over her shoulder at her friend, tormenting him with a flash of her nape.

"Thanks. I owe you." She turned back to him and stilled. "What?"

He brushed trembling fingers up her neck and couldn't stop himself from uttering, "What's this all about?"

The nerves he was battling grew worse when a look entered her eyes, one that told him he wasn't going crazy and he had been right to think her pinning her hair up had been intentional.

Gods.

He swallowed hard.

"You look spooked again," she whispered and sidled closer to him.

His eyes darted between hers. "You're sure? Like really sure? You should think about it, because if we do this—"

"I've been thinking about it for weeks, Knox, and the answer never changes. I want to be with you. I want this." She stroked a hand down his chest.

A sudden urge to growl and seize hold of her swept through him and he gritted his teeth, his lips drawing back in a grimace as the need to mate with her before she could change her mind took control of him, only it was miles of driving and a long walk to his cabin.

Skye slipped her hand into his and tugged him towards the door to the left of the bar, one that led upstairs to her apartment.

Stacy shook her head and kept polishing the glasses as Skye pulled him past her. "At least keep it down this time. Last time you almost gave old McGregor a heart attack."

A blush stained Skye's cheeks.

Might have heated his too.

He wasn't sure he could keep the noise down this time either. Already the urge to mate with Skye was stealing control of him, had him hard in his jeans and aching to be inside her. His fangs dropped, mouth watering at the thought of sinking them into her nape.

She opened the door and he grabbed her, scooped her up into his arms and took the stairs two at a time. He crossed her small living area to her bedroom and dropped her on the bed, made fast work of her clothes as his heart thundered, blood rushing as it heated. Her little moan as he tossed her boots and jeans aside and pulled her top off, revealing her body to his hungry gaze, urged him on together with the scent of her desire and how flushed her cheeks were.

She wanted this. Really wanted this.

Knox shed his own clothes, not slowing even as Skye raked her gaze over him, silently devouring every inch of his body with it, making him wild for her. She removed her bra and threw it aside with a sultry smile on her lips, a wicked glint in her eyes that dared him to come and get her.

When she stroked her fingers down her neck, he growled and bared fangs, half of him expecting her to grow fearful at the sight of them. She didn't. Her heated look only grew more intense, more hungry, scalded him and had his cock rock hard.

She dropped her hands to her panties.

On a low growl, he grabbed her, flipped her onto her knees at the edge of the mattress and tore them away. He snarled as he filled her in one thrust, claiming her body, tried to convince himself to be gentle with her but it was impossible as his gaze landed on her nape.

Knox drove into her, clutching her hip with one hand to keep her in place and running his other one down the line of her spine.

He stared down at her as he filled her, his gaze tracking over her curves, her scent making him wild as he fought to calm his racing heart and remain in control. He wanted this to feel good for her, wanted it to be a moment neither of them would ever forget. Her pleasure trickled into him through the fragile bond that had been slowly growing between them and he groaned as she rocked back against him, taking him deep into her whenever he withdrew. He could sense her need, couldn't hold back the growl as the urge to pleasure her stole command of him, the need to satisfy his female a powerful drug that forced him to obey it.

She moaned, the breathless little sound teasing his ears as he stroked her deeper, harder, lowered his gaze and watched his rigid cock sliding into her with each powerful thrust. Gods. He groaned and gripped her harder, his instincts roaring to life to sweep him up in them as he took her, as he looked at what he was doing and how his shaft glistened with her arousal. Need rolled through him, twisting him tight inside, until he was sure he couldn't breathe.

He needed more.

He needed all of her.

On a low growl, he grabbed her right breast and pulled her up to him, bent his knees to keep himself inside her and stared at her nape, his rough breaths bouncing back at him as he thrust into her. She moaned and writhed, her keening cries gaining volume and pitch as he drove into her welcoming heat, as she tightened around him and he sensed how close she was.

She lifted her arms and draped them over his shoulders, and he groaned as she cupped his nape, as she held on to it as he took her. He savoured her sweet cries as he shifted his left hand to the apex of her thighs and stroked her between them, fondling her bundle of nerves.

Her body kicked forwards as she cried out and trembled around his length, milking it in a demanding way that had the need blazing within him growing stronger, had him pushing her through the haze of one release and towards another as he stared at her nape, as he lost himself in the moment. She moaned and clutched him, rotated her hips and drove him mad, pushing him to the very edge.

On a feral snarl, Knox angled his head and sank his fangs into her nape, gripped her hard and kept her in place with his bite as he drove into her, as he thrust harder and deeper, claiming all of her. The first drop of her blood on his tongue had fire raging through him, had the world dropping away as something altered inside him, as everything changed in a heartbeat.

Her feelings flooded him, her pleasure mingling with his, growing stronger by the second as the bond formed between them, linking them deeply, allowing her to feel everything he did too.

Sweet gods.

Stars winked across the darkness of his closed eyes as his release rolled up on him like a tidal wave, as it broke over him and almost broke him in the process. Every inch of him quivered in time with Skye, trembled as fiercely as her body was as she broke apart again, as his cock kicked and throbbed inside her. He released her nape, managed a single swipe of his tongue over the puncture wounds to steal the pain away.

And then collapsed to his knees.

"Knox!" Skye turned towards him in an instant, dropping to all fours, her beautiful flushed face awash with concern.

He swallowed hard and struggled to breathe as he continued to shake, as pleasure rocked him and refused to release him, was sure he looked like an idiot or weak to her.

She slipped from the bed onto his lap, wrapped her arms around him and kissed him, lightly stroking her lips across his. Distracting him. Calming him. He sank into that kiss, drowned in the feelings it held, in the ones he could sense in their connection as it slowly finished forming.

A bond that was forever.

His beautiful mate continued to hold him, eased him down and pieced him back together, gazed at him with affection and not judgement in her eyes as she finally drew back to look at him. She feathered her fingers across his damp brow, down his cheek, her look one of concern now.

"That was intense." She smiled for him, one that stole his heart.

"A little more than I was expecting." But he should have known it would wreck him, that mating with her would do this to him, affecting him this deeply, because in his heart he had known that the love they shared was endless, deeper than normal love, the sort that led to a powerful mating.

A powerful bond.

She kissed him again and he took control this time, wanting her to see that he was strong, that his moment of weakness was over, even when he knew it wasn't. She had a way of making him weak, and he loved it.

Time trickled past as he kissed her, as he savoured the connection between them, and slowly his thoughts turned to Black Ridge and how the planned get-together was looking more like a party now. A celebration.

Skye finally stood and he growled as he watched her walking into her bathroom, as he stared at the marks on the nape of her neck.

His marks.

His mate.

He stood on trembling legs and dressed, sank onto the edge of the mattress as Skye moved around the room. He tracked her with his gaze, enjoying the way she glanced at him from time to time as she dressed, a shy edge to her dark eyes.

He wasn't sure there was a bear in all the world as happy as he was right now.

When she finished dressing, donning her blue jeans and a pretty black flowing camisole that had purple flowers stitched onto it, she came to him. Kissed him. He groaned and kissed her back, getting fired up again.

He tried to tug her onto the bed with him but she twirled out of his grip.

"Come on. I don't want to be late." She untied her hair, letting it fall around her shoulders, hiding his mark.

He huffed and stood, followed her back down the stairs and vowed that he would make love with her later, when they were alone in his cabin, assuaging his need to satisfy his mate.

When they reached the bottom of the stairs, she was quick to scurry towards the main door of the bar, keeping her head down. Knox strode through it with his shoulders tipped back and his head held high. A few of the males tossed him looks, some of them disgusted while others looked as if they wanted to congratulate him on a job well done.

He glared at those men, because he didn't like the thought of them imagining his female naked, bucking against him, wild in the throes of passion.

He strode after Skye on legs that were still a little unsteady and caught up with her on the deck of the bar.

Paused and stared at her.

Still couldn't believe she was his mate now even when he could feel it in every beat of his heart.

She looped her arm around his and smiled up at him, her eyes bright with the pleasure he could feel in her, the contentment. Those feelings ran through him too, had him smiling down at her as he lost himself in her eyes, in their bond.

"Looks like it'll be another busy day at the bar." He dragged his gaze away from hers and noted that more of the outside tables were occupied now.

"Thanks again for helping me out." She tiptoed and he leaned towards her, wanting that kiss on his cheek.

"What's mine is yours, Skye. All of it." He glanced back at the bar as he led her towards his truck. "I love this place too and I'll do whatever it takes to keep it open. I know how important it is to you, so it's important to me too."

She smiled. "And that's why I love you."

Knox missed a step.

Grinned at her.

"You love me?"

That was the first time she had said it.

Before she could say a word, only blush, he said, "I love you too."

He swept her up into his arms and kissed her, an all-too-brief one that only got him fired up again, and set her down. She seized his hand and led him along the street, past his truck.

"Where are we going?" He looked back at the pickup. "I'm parked right there."

"I should bring something for the party tonight." She glanced over her shoulder at him.

He figured she meant something like wine or a soda, a token gesture of thanks to the host of the get-together.

Only she led him to the store and ordered a lot of steaks.

When the cashier totalled it up, she looked at him. "What's yours is mine, right?"

He chuckled and kissed her, slipped his arm around her waist and his other hand into his pocket for his wallet.

"Oh, and I'll take that tray too." She leaned right, away from him, and he tried to see what she was pointing at.

He wasn't surprised when the woman behind the counter pulled a whole tray of brownies out and started boxing them up. Skye had discovered a dangerous way into the hearts of everyone at Black Ridge a few months back when she had brought brownies for everyone. It turned out that keeping the females happy with chocolate had made her very popular with Saint and Lowe.

And had revealed that Rune and Maverick both had a sweet tooth.

Knox paid for her purchases and took the heavy bags for her, led her to his truck and put them in the cooler in the back. He opened her door for her and she smiled as she hopped up into the cab. He rounded the vehicle and slid into the driver's seat, and tried hard to resist gunning the engine and seeing just how quickly he could get her back to his cabin.

The journey was agonising—every second cramped into the small space with her driving him wild with a need to kiss her at the very least. He did just that when they reached the trailhead, pinned her to the side of the truck and took his time about it, savouring the way she moaned and arched into him, how he could feel the pleasure she took from his kiss and how much she loved him.

Knox locked the truck and grabbed the cooler, and Skye's hand. The afternoon was wearing on by the time they finally neared home, following the creek. Voices sounded through the trees and Rath came into view, standing on the stony edge of the water, a fishing rod in hand.

Ivy poked her head out from behind her mate, her hazel eyes warm and bright as they landed on him and Skye.

Rath glanced at him too, reeled in his line and turned towards him. "Nice day for a walk."

"Summer is finally here. Planning to enjoy it too." Knox lifted the cooler. "Party at the Ridge tonight. Skye bought an insane amount of steaks and brownies with my money."

She beamed at the cougar and his mate. "Come along. The more the merrier. We're celebrating!"

Knox couldn't hold back his grin as he glanced down at her and saw the happiness in her eyes.

"Oh, you mated!" Ivy came around Rath and swept Skye into a tight hug. "Congratulations! You are going to love it. Being mated... wow... just wow. You'd think they'd get less intense, but nope... they get more intense."

Rath scowled at his mate's back, his grey eyes holding a hint of gold that told Knox the cougar alpha wasn't angry with her, he was hungry for her. Probably thinking about their mating.

"We'll be there." Rath was quick to grab his mate, pull her away from Skye and into his arms.

Knox growled, wanting to do that with Skye, but she tugged on his hand, pulling him towards the Ridge. He obeyed, trailed behind her as she picked up pace now, as her excitement flowed through him.

The cabins of Black Ridge came into view and he spotted Lowe already setting up the fire pit and the grill.

"Skye brought more meat," Knox hollered and held the cooler aloft as Lowe looked at him.

His twin froze.

Smiled from ear to ear.

Knox should have known that his twin would be able to sense the change in him, just as he had been able to sense it when Lowe had finally mated with Cameo.

"You mated!" Lowe took swift strides to him, shouted that loud enough that Saint came out of his cabin.

"They mated?" Saint looked at Knox and then Skye. "Thank the gods. No more moody Knox growling and prowling around the Ridge."

Knox shot his alpha a look. He hadn't been moody. Well, he hadn't been that moody. Maybe a little moody.

Cameo and Holly came and stole Skye from him.

"Congratulations." Holly snuck a glance at her mate, Saint, her grey eyes sparkling with that same cougar gold that had been in Rath's eyes. She flicked her black hair over her shoulder and Saint growled, looked as if he wanted to whisk her away into his cabin.

Instead, his alpha ran a hand over his dark hair and strode towards him and Lowe. Saint clapped a hand down on Knox's shoulder.

"Congratulations." His dark eyes revealed how deeply Saint meant that and Knox clasped his shoulder.

"Thanks." He watched his new mate as Cameo grabbed her a beer from the ice pail near the logs that formed seats around the firepit and handed it to her.

The females clinked their bottles together in a toast that had Skye grinning from ear to ear.

Had Knox smiling too.

Cameo's blue eyes were bright with happiness and affection as they talked, her brown-to-blonde hair tied up to reveal her own mating marks on her nape. He remembered how relieved he had been when he had sensed the shift in Lowe's mood and had realised he and Cameo had mated, could see in Lowe's blue eyes when he glanced at him that that feeling ran through him too. His brother was happy for him, pleased that he finally had his mate.

Knox went back to watching Skye and couldn't stop himself from thinking about the fact he and his twin were similar in another way too— he didn't want her to give up her dream to be with him. He knew how important her bar was to her and that meant he was going to be splitting his time between Black Ridge and town, just like Lowe split his time between it and the place where Cameo had rented a small bolthole.

Cameo was determined to continue doing her job as a ranger for as long as she could before people began noticing she was barely ageing now thanks to the bond she had with Lowe. She had managed to move to a position closer to Black Ridge, but still had to spend weekdays staying in her rented home so she could get to work.

Knox missed his brother in the weeks where he stayed with his mate. He glanced at Skye again. Maybe she could keep him distracted. In fact, there was no *maybe* about it. All he needed to do was time his stays at her place so they coincided with Lowe staying with Cameo and he would be so swept up in his mate that he would forget about missing his brother.

"I know that look," Lowe grunted, gaining his attention. His brother shot him a smile. "You'll still miss me... believe me."

Lowe always had been able to read him.

He felt better about it when Lowe patted Knox's shoulder.

"I always miss you too." Lowe took the cooler from him and started towards the females. "Gods know why... although you might be more bearable now you're mated."

Saint chuckled.

Knox scowled at Lowe's back and stalked after his twin. "Yeah, well, life with you has hardly been all peaches and cream. I got to remind you how grouchy you were before you finally mated?"

Cameo raised her beer in the air. "You don't have to remind me. I was there!"

The females erupted in giggles and Saint chuckled again as Lowe huffed.

Saint slapped Knox on the back, jerking him forwards, towards his brother. "You'll both still miss each other, and for some godsdamned reason I'll miss you both too. The Ridge is just too damned quiet when both of you aren't around."

Knox hadn't even thought about how his alpha felt about him and Lowe being away from the pride. He glanced at Saint and then turned to him, lifted his hand and gripped his shoulder as he smiled at him, hoping to reassure him that both he and Lowe would be safe and they would be careful too. Nothing would happen to them.

Besides, he had the feeling that it would be sooner rather than later that Cameo and Skye ended up moving to Black Ridge, although if Skye did that, she could still work at her bar. He looked over his shoulder at them. Both females looked incredibly at home as they stood near the firepit in the middle of the clearing and laughed at something Holly had said.

His heart warmed at the sight of Skye.

She turned to him, her dark eyes lighting up with her smile, and he growled low as she came to him, her hips kicking with each step, stoking his hunger. He swept her into his arms and kissed her, eliciting another cheer from everyone present, and then led her to one of the logs.

Cameo followed them and handed Knox a beer and he eased down onto a log beside Skye. He thanked her by tipping the bottle towards her and grew deeply aware of Skye as she leaned into his side, as she laughed and talked, as her happiness filled him too.

Afternoon turned to evening, and Maverick and Rune joined them, congratulated him and Skye and then made off with two of the brownies Holly had set out on a table for dessert. She chased after them, chastising them, causing Saint to chuckle.

Saint looked towards the Creek and Knox looked there too. He smiled when he saw Rath and everyone coming out of the woods. The four cougar brothers had relaxed a lot over the past few months, the uneasy truce between Black Ridge and Cougar Creek becoming a solid friendship that often saw them visiting each other to pass an evening like this.

As night fell, the smell of steaks had Knox's stomach growling. He rubbed at it, his mouth watering at the thought of them as he watched Lowe working his magic.

A howl cut through the darkness.

Everyone fell silent.

Rune stiffened and looked off towards the woods behind Knox, on the other side of the creek.

And then he was gone.

"What—?" Skye twisted, looked in the direction Rune had sprinted and then back at Knox.

Her nerves ran into him through their bond.

He took hold of her hand as the wolf howled again, as she tensed and turned a fearful look on the dark trees across the creek. "Rune will be fine. He just really hates wolves. He'll chase it off so we're all safe and then he'll be back."

Saint looked at Maverick.

Maverick nodded and gave chase.

"The way you said that... Was that a regular wolf... or are there werewolves up here too?" She cast another glance at the woods.

Knox slid his arm around her shoulder and tucked her against him, making her look at him again.

"The wolves live in the valley next door. Run a lodge there." Saint came to sit on the other side of her and Knox appreciated the hell out of the male reassuring his mate and making her feel safe and protected.

Her voice gained pitch.

"Wait? White Wolf Lodge? The tourist cabins?" Before anyone could answer that, she shrugged it off. "I'm starting to see this world in a whole new light."

Knox tugged her closer to him and she glanced at him, lingered as their eyes met. "Welcome to my crazy world."

She smiled. "Our crazy world."

Looked as if she wanted to kiss him.

"Honey-bourbon-glazed steaks are ready," Lowe announced.

Knox groaned, torn between kissing her and grabbing one before the others could. Skye must have felt the war within him, the pain caused by the thought of everyone but him getting their hands on the delicious, sweet steaks that he was sure Lowe had made just for him, a special treat to celebrate his mating, because she frowned at him.

"You really should keep a hive if you love honey that much." Her eyes widened. "Oh my God. I just got why you have a honey obsession. You're a bear!"

Everyone laughed.

Even Skye.

Her eyes lit up with it, with the love he could feel in her. His female. His mate. His Skye.

Knox growled and silenced her with a kiss.

Might have thought about drizzling her with honey and bourbon and licking it off her.

The End

ABOUT THE AUTHOR

Felicity Heaton is a New York Times and USA Today best-selling author who writes passionate paranormal romance books. In her books she creates detailed worlds, twisting plots, mind-blowing action, intense emotion and heart-stopping romances with leading men that vary from dark deadly vampires to sexy shape-shifters and wicked werewolves, to sinful angels and hot demons!

If you're a fan of paranormal romance authors Lara Adrian, J R Ward, Sherrilyn Kenyon, Kresley Cole, Gena Showalter, Larissa Ione and Christine Feehan then you will enjoy her books too.

If you love your angels a little dark and wicked, her best-selling Her Angel romance series is for you. If you like strong, powerful, and dark vampires then try the Vampires Realm romance series or any of her stand alone vampire romance books. If you're looking for vampire romances that are sinful, passionate and erotic then try her London Vampires romance series. Or if you like hot-blooded alpha heroes who will let nothing stand in the way of them claiming their destined woman then try her Eternal Mates series. It's packed with sexy heroes in a world populated by elves, vampires, fae, demons, shifters, and more. If sexy Greek gods with incredible powers battling to save our world and their home in the Underworld are more your thing, then be sure to step into the world of Guardians of Hades.

If you have enjoyed this story, please take a moment to contact the author at **author@felicityheaton.com** or to post a review of the book online

Connect with Felicity:
Website – http://www.felicityheaton.com
Blog – http://www.felicityheaton.com/blog/
Twitter – http://twitter.com/felicityheaton
Facebook – http://www.facebook.com/felicityheaton
Goodreads – http://www.goodreads.com/felicityheaton
Mailing List – http://www.felicityheaton.com/newsletter.php

FIND OUT MORE ABOUT HER BOOKS AT:
http://www.felicityheaton.com

Made in the USA
Coppell, TX
22 February 2024

29295970R00102